TWO DATES FOR THE DANCE . . .

Melanie glanced at Scott out of the corner of her eye. He was one of the cutest boys in the seventh grade. Not only that, he *liked* her. A rush of guilt filled her heart. How could she possibly hurt someone as special as Scott?

When she closed her locker and looked back at him, he was still smiling.

"Say, Mel. Would you like to go to the Valentine party at Bumpers with me?" he asked.

Like a runaway elevator, Melanie's stomach dropped toward her shoes. The moment she had been dreading had arrived, and Scott was actually asking her to the party. She was going to have to turn him down. There was no choice. She already had a date with Shane.

She took a deep breath. "Gosh . . . Scott . . ." she finally managed to get out. "I'd . . . love . . . to . . . but . . ."

The rest of her words were drowned out by the bell.

Scott's eyes lit up. "You'd love to! Great! I've got to go. I'll talk to you later." He whirled around and disappeared in the crowd of kids pushing their way to classes.

"Wait!" Melanie shouted, but it was too late. . . .

Bantam Skylark Books by Betsy Haynes
Ask your bookseller for the books you have missed

THE AGAINST TAFFY SINCLAIR CLUB
TAFFY SINCLAIR STRIKES AGAIN
TAFFY SINCLAIR, QUEEN OF THE SOAPS
TAFFY SINCLAIR AND THE ROMANCE MACHINE DISASTER
BLACKMAILED BY TAFFY SINCLAIR
TAFFY SINCLAIR, BABY ASHLEY, AND ME
TAFFY SINCLAIR AND THE SECRET ADMIRER EPIDEMIC
TAFFY SINCLAIR AND THE MELANIE MAKE-OVER
THE TRUTH ABOUT TAFFY SINCLAIR
TAFFY SINCLAIR GOES TO HOLLYWOOD
THE GREAT MOM SWAP
THE GREAT BOYFRIEND TRAP

Books in The Fabulous Five Series

1 SEVENTH-GRADE RUMORS
2 THE TROUBLE WITH FLIRTING
3 THE POPULARITY TRAP
4 HER HONOR, KATIE SHANNON
5 THE BRAGGING WAR
6 THE PARENT GAME
7 THE KISSING DISASTER
8 THE RUNAWAY CRISIS
9 THE BOYFRIEND DILEMMA
#10 PLAYING THE PART
#11 HIT AND RUN
#12 KATIE'S DATING TIPS
#13 THE CHRISTMAS COUNTDOWN
#14 SEVENTH-GRADE MENACE
#15 MELANIE'S IDENTITY CRISIS
#16 THE HOT-LINE EMERGENCY
#17 TEEN TAXI
#18 CELEBRITY AUCTION
#19 THE BOYS-ONLY CLUB
#20 THE WITCHES OF WAKEMAN
#21 JANA TO THE RESCUE
#22 MELANIE'S VALENTINE

The Fabulous Five Super Editions
#1 THE FABULOUS FIVE IN TROUBLE
#2 CARIBBEAN ADVENTURE

THE FABULOUS FIVE

Melanie's Valentine

BETSY HAYNES

A BANTAM SKYLARK BOOK®
NEW YORK • TORONTO • SYDNEY • AUCKLAND

RL 5, 009–012

MELANIE'S VALENTINE
A Bantam Skylark Book / February 1991

Skylark Books is a registered trademark of Bantam Books, a division of Bantam Doubleday Dell Publishing Group, Inc. Registered in U.S. Patent and Trademark Office and elsewhere.

ISBN 0-553-15845-7

Published simultaneously in the United States and Canada

Bantam Books are published by Bantam Books, a division of Bantam Doubleday Dell Publishing Group, Inc. Its trademark, consisting of the words "Bantam Books" and the portrayal of a rooster, is Registered in U.S. Patent and Trademark Office and in other countries. Marca Registrada. Bantam Books, 666 Fifth Avenue, New York, New York 10103.

PRINTED IN THE UNITED STATES OF AMERICA

CWO 0 9 8 7 6 5 4 3 2 1

Melanie's Valentine

CHAPTER

1

"Melanie, honey, let's go over this list. There are lots of things I want you to be sure to remember while your grandmother's here," Mrs. Edwards called from the kitchen just as Melanie headed up the stairs to her room. "She'll be arriving in the morning, you know."

Melanie stopped in the middle of the stairway, but she didn't turn around.

"Mo-*om*," she protested. "I already know all that stuff. Besides, Shane will be here in less than an hour, and I haven't even decided what I'm going to wear yet."

"I know how important your big date with Shane

is, but this will just take a moment," her mother said firmly.

Melanie rolled her eyes and trudged back down the stairs. Sometimes she was sure that either her mother had been born already an adult or else she had amnesia about being in the seventh grade. Otherwise, she'd remember what it was like. And she'd understand how important it was to be going to the varsity basketball game with Shane Arrington, who was the cutest, the coolest, the most laid-back boy in Wakeman Junior High.

"Now, I want you to remember to keep your stereo turned low enough so that it doesn't disturb Grandma Dee . . ."

"I know, I know," insisted Melanie, "and don't hog the bathroom. We've been over all this a hundred times. Why don't you just give me the list and let me tape it up in the middle of my mirror?"

"Great idea," her mother said brightly, holding the list out toward her.

Melanie groaned under her breath and took it. Couldn't her mother tell when she was just kidding?

When she got to her room, Melanie started to toss the list onto her desk, but her conscience was nagging at her. Instead, she got out her tape and centered the list in the mirror above her dresser. She knew it would please her mom if she came into the room and saw it. She hadn't meant to be so crabby. And she really was glad that Grandma Dee was coming to stay with them for a while. It was just that this was such an important night.

She had had a crush on Shane Arrington ever since their first day at Wakeman Junior High. He had always been friendly and sometimes acted as if he liked her, too. But it wasn't until she'd followed the instructions in the love test that her cousin from California had sent her that Shane had liked her enough to ask her out.

Melanie smiled to herself as she remembered how the love test had almost ended in disaster. She had done everything her cousin had told her to do to make Shane her one true love. She had handed out copies of the test to six girls, waited four days, and then drunk a glass of water and started to say Shane's name, which was supposed to make her romance come true.

But it was just then that that jerk Richie Corrierro had stuck a rubber frog in her face and yelled, "Kiss me—I'm a prince!" And instead of saying Shane's name, she had done something absolutely awful. She had screamed, "*Richie!*" From that instant on, she had been sure she was doomed to spend the rest of her life dodging Richie Corrierro. But somehow, even without her saying Shane's name, the love test had worked, and he had asked her to go to the basketball game tonight.

Melanie sighed and threw herself across her bed to dream about Shane, but then she bounced straight up again as she caught sight of the clock on her bedside table.

"Oh, my gosh! He'll be here in half an hour!"

Twenty-nine and a half minutes later, she came tearing back down the stairs. Shane was here. She had seen his father's ancient orange Volkswagen Bug with flowers and butterflies painted on the sides sitting in the driveway beside her mother's red van.

"Mom! Dad! I'm going! I'll be home early!" she shouted as she grabbed her coat and tried to catch her breath. She opened the front door just as Shane was raising a fist to knock.

"Oh, hi," she said, suddenly feeling shy.

"Hi," said Shane, giving her an easy smile that made her knees turn to putty. "Ready to go?"

She nodded, and they climbed into the backseat of the VW Bug. Mr. Arrington nodded hello from the front seat and backed the car into traffic, heading for the junior high gym. With his winter coat buttoned up, it was hard to tell that Shane's father was a former hippie, who still wore mostly jeans and sweatshirts with hand-painted peace signs on them.

Melanie racked her brain for something to say. It was always awkward to try to make conversation with a boy in front of one of his parents.

"Did I tell you that my grandma is coming to stay with us for a while?" she asked over the sputter and chug of the ancient car. "She's coming tomorrow, and she'll be here at least a month."

"Really? That's nice. Where does she live?" asked

Shane, and Melanie was amazed that he seemed genuinely interested.

"Florida," she said. "But she's not like all those *retired* people who live in Florida. She's really neat. She does fun things like waterskiing and scuba diving. Last month she wrote me that she'd been parasailing!"

"Hey, she sounds terrific," said Shane. "I can't wait to meet her."

Melanie swallowed hard. *Shane wanted to meet her grandmother?* Maybe he *did* know he was her one true love, after all. Usually boys didn't talk about meeting girls' grandmothers unless they planned to practically become part of the family.

Just then Shane's father pulled the Bug up to the curb in front of the gym. Melanie thanked him for the ride as she and Shane got out.

The line to get into the game between the Wakeman Warriors and the Black Rock Buccaneers was half a block long, but Melanie didn't mind. Usually she wasn't a show-off, but tonight she was glad that everyone would see her standing outside the gymnasium with Shane Arrington and know they were on a date together. It made her tingle with excitement to think how many girls would like to be in her place.

"Want some popcorn?" Shane asked nonchalantly when they finally got inside.

"Sure," said Melanie. "The concession stand looks crowded. I'll wait for you here."

"Hi, Mel!" came a chorus of voices from behind her as soon as Shane had walked away. Melanie knew before she turned around that the voices belonged to her friends in The Fabulous Five, and she waved happily to Jana Morgan, Katie Shannon, and Christie Winchell, noticing that Beth Barry wasn't with them. The Fabulous Five had been very best friends since elementary school, and they almost always did everything together.

"Hi, guys!" she sang out. "Come here a minute."

She was bouncing up and down with excitement as her three friends approached. "Can you believe this! I'm really on a date with Shane!" she gushed before any of them could say a word. "Doesn't he look handsome? I can't *believe* this is really happening!"

"Well, I believe it," Christie assured her. "And so does everybody else. You should have heard some of the girls in the ticket line. They were so jealous of you that they were about to die."

"Right," said Jana. "You two were just about the only thing anyone was talking about."

Melanie beamed at her friends. "That's music to my ears," she said. Then, frowning, she added, "Where's Beth? Didn't she come to the game tonight?"

"She's working at the concession stand," said Katie. "It's the Drama Club's turn tonight. She said she could probably sit with us after the half, though."

Melanie nodded. The school allowed a different

club to work at the refreshment stand during each home game, and the profits from that night's sales went into that club's treasury.

"Speaking of the concession stand," Katie said in a confidential voice, "would you look who's waiting on Shane."

Melanie shot a glance toward the stand. The crowd had thinned enough for her to see into it. Unfortunately, Beth was on the other side waiting on a customer, because she could see Shane leaning against the counter and waiting for his order as Laura McCall hurried toward him, giving him a flirty grin. To Melanie's horror, Shane was grinning back.

"That rat!" Melanie said between clenched teeth. "Shane's *my* date. What does she think she's doing?"

Jana sighed. "Oh, you know Laura."

"Right," said Katie. "She's only happy when she's making trouble for one of The Fabulous Five."

"*And* trying to steal someone else's boyfriend," added Christie. "I don't know why Mr. Levine lets her be in Drama Club anyway. The Halloween production proved she couldn't act."

Melanie nodded, keeping track of Laura out of the corner of her eye. "Look at that," she muttered. "Laura's the biggest flirt in the entire world."

Now Laura was holding out a box of popcorn, but each time Shane reached for it, she laughed and pulled it away.

"How disgusting," said Katie.

"Uh-oh. Here he comes," whispered Christie.

"See you later, Mel," said Jana as she and the others turned toward the bleachers.

Melanie watched her friends go as half a dozen emotions battled it out inside her. This was supposed to be her big date with Shane. The most fabulous night of her life. So should she let Shane know that she had seen him flirting with Laura McCall and that she was angry? Or should she just act innocent and pretend that she hadn't seen a thing? Why did Laura McCall have to spoil things by waiting on him in the first place? Why couldn't it have been Dekeisha or one of her own best friends, Beth Barry?

She glanced at him as he sauntered toward her, a box of popcorn in each hand. He was smiling at her, looking cool as usual, and she could feel the thumping of her heart grow louder and louder inside her chest. Surely she had been imagining things. Or had she?

CHAPTER 2

"This place is filling up fast," Shane said. "We'd better get a seat. I told some of the Riverfield kids that we'd sit with them."

"Riverfield?" Melanie asked in surprise. She and The Fabulous Five always sat with their friends from Mark Twain Elementary. Of course, Shane had gone to Riverfield Elementary, but so had Laura McCall and the rest of The Fantastic Foursome, The Fabulous Five's biggest rivals. Was Laura why he wanted to sit with that crowd?

"Sure. Why not? Hey, there's Bill Soliday and Tony Sanchez waving at us. They said they'd save us some seats."

Shane took her arm and steered her in the direction of the Riverfield section. Melanie looked helplessly toward her friends from Mark Twain. Katie and Jana had started to wave in her direction, too, but let their arms fall back to their sides in disappointment when they saw Melanie and Shane heading up the bleachers toward the other group of kids. Melanie saw Scott Daly sitting with the Mark Twain kids, too, and looked away quickly before he spotted her. Scott had been her unofficial boyfriend since sixth grade. She still liked him, but not as much as she liked Shane.

The first half of the game went quickly, and Melanie almost forgot about Laura's flirting with Shane. She was glad that it was a varsity game and she and the other seventh-grade cheerleaders weren't on the floor. Usually Melanie loved being with the squad, but tonight she had fun yelling for the team and doing cheers with Shane and the rest of the crowd.

When the buzzer sounded for the half, Shane jumped to his feet. "Want something to drink?" he asked. "They've got ice cream, too."

A stab of jealousy went through Melanie as she thought of Laura at the concession stand, but Shane had been so much fun during the game that she brushed it aside. "A cola," she answered.

As soon as he was gone, Katie, Christie, and Jana slid across the bleacher seats to join her.

"We're going down to keep an eye on Laura," said Christie. "Want to come along?"

"I don't know," said Melanie. "If Shane saw me, he'd know I was spying."

"No, he wouldn't," insisted Jana. "You could just say you were going to the girls' room with us to comb your hair."

Melanie made a face. She wasn't sure how convincing that story would be, especially if Shane caught her standing around watching the refreshment stand. Still, she was dying to know what Laura would do when Shane came back for drinks.

"Okay," she said. "But you guys have to help me out if Shane sees me."

"Hey, we're The Fabulous Five," Katie reminded her with a wink. "Best friends forever, right?"

Melanie hung behind her friends as they headed toward the front of the gym. Maybe if Shane looked her way, she could duck behind them.

The refreshment stand was crowded again, but Melanie managed to spot Shane as he inched his way to the counter.

"Oh, come on, Beth or Dekeisha. Please wait on Shane before Laura sees him," she pleaded softly.

"Would you look at that!" Katie snorted. "There goes Laura."

Melanie narrowed her eyes and watched Laura make a beeline toward Shane. But fortunately, Beth got there ahead of Laura. Melanie and her friends exchanged glances of relief. Still, she couldn't stand to watch anymore. "I'm going back to my seat," she mumbled.

"Don't worry. We'll keep an eye on Laura," said Christie. She gave Melanie a sympathetic look.

How could tonight be turning out so awful? Melanie wondered as she headed back to the bleachers. Shane is supposed to be my one true love. So why was he flirting with Laura McCall?

Just then she felt a soft tap on her shoulder. Turning around, she was surprised to see that it was Scott Daly.

"Hi, Mel," he said. "I didn't know you were here. Why aren't you sitting with your friends?"

Melanie gulped hard. Apparently Scott hadn't seen her come in with Shane after all. As far as he knew, she might be here with some girls. Her mind started whirling. If Shane was her true love, then she wouldn't be going out with Scott anymore. But Shane was flirting with Laura. Maybe after tonight he would never ask her out again, and she would be glad that Scott still liked her.

Melanie crossed her fingers behind her back. "Oh, I'm sitting with some kids from Riverfield," she said, feeling terrible for telling only part of the truth.

"Okay . . . Well, I'll see you around," Scott said.

Melanie breathed a sigh of relief and turned to go up to her seat when she had the eerie feeling that someone was looking at her. She knew who it was before she even looked his way. Shane was standing not four feet away with a drink in each hand and a questioning look on his face.

Oh, no! thought Melanie, trying not to panic. He saw me talking to Scott. What if he thinks *I* was the one doing the flirting?

Shane's eyes flicked toward Scott, but he didn't say anything. He just handed Melanie her cola, and they went back to their seats in silence.

The awkward silence hung between them through the rest of the game. A hundred times Melanie started to turn to Shane and ask him what was wrong, but each time she lost her nerve. Instead, she watched him out of the corner of her eye and prayed that he would say something to her. A couple of times she thought he was going to. But he didn't.

Was he mad at her for talking to Scott? Or was he sorry he had come to the game with her instead of Laura? The questions churned in Melanie's mind. But worse than that was the big ache in her heart.

The Arringtons' Technicolor Volkswagen was waiting by the curb when they left the gym after the game. Melanie ducked into the backseat with Shane, and the car sped away.

They rode along in silence for a few blocks, and then Shane leaned close and whispered to her over the noise of the engine, "I saw you talking to Scott Daly. He's your old boyfriend, isn't he?"

Melanie was startled. "So, don't accuse me of anything. I saw *you* flirting with Laura McCall."

"Flirting?" Shane burst out. "I wasn't *flirting* with Laura. But maybe you were flirting with Scott. Is that it?"

"Of course not," Melanie insisted. "Scott and I are just good friends."

"But you used to go out, didn't you?"

Melanie nodded, but she didn't say anything.

"Well, I've never gone out with Laura. No matter what you think, I like you."

"You do?" Melanie whispered. She thought her heart would burst.

"Sure. Laura's okay, but that's all."

Melanie wanted to laugh. She wanted to giggle, and bounce up and down on the seat, and shout how happy she was. Instead, she smiled at Shane as sweetly as she could and said, "That's the same way I feel about Scott. He's okay, but I like you, too."

Shane took her hand. Then he leaned toward her in the dark backseat and kissed her.

CHAPTER

3

"Melanie! Time to get up!"

Melanie slowly opened her eyes and then closed them tightly again when she realized that it was morning and her mother was calling.

"Go away," she muttered, pulling the pillow over her head. It had taken forever to get to sleep last night after her date with Shane and their kiss in the backseat of the Volkswagen Bug. And just now she had been having the most delicious dream about Shane. They had been walking hand in hand along a beautiful beach when her mother had to call her and interrupt everything.

Mrs. Edwards poked her head in the door. "Come on, sweetheart. It's time to get up. We have to go to the airport this morning to meet your grandmother Dee's plane from Florida."

Oh, no. Not this morning, Melanie thought. Why does it have to be this morning? All I want to do is lie here and dream about Shane.

Just then Jeffy, her six-year-old brother, zoomed into the room with his arms spread wide, making noises like a jet airplane. "Come on, Mel!" he shouted between buzzing sounds. "It's time to go!"

Slowly Melanie dragged herself out of bed. It was no use. She would have to put her dreaming on hold and get up. Throwing on jeans and a ski sweater and giving her hair a quick brushing, she hurried down to the kitchen and grabbed a cup of strawberry-banana yogurt out of the refrigerator.

Mrs. Edwards was standing at the sink, rinsing dishes and putting them into the dishwasher. She glanced over her shoulder at Melanie and smiled. "I didn't get a chance to talk much with you when you came in last night. How was your date with Shane?"

Shane's kiss flooded Melanie's mind, and she could feel herself blushing. "Great," she said, suddenly getting interested in her yogurt, in the hope that her mother wouldn't be able to see how red her face was. "We really had fun."

"That's nice, dear. Who won the game?"

Melanie blinked. She didn't have the slightest idea who had won the game. She had been too worried about Shane's silence to notice the score or even pay attention to which side was cheering the loudest. "Uhm . . . I forget," she said lamely.

Her mother chuckled. "Well, one thing's certain. You have a bigger crush on Shane Arrington than you ever had on Scott Daly."

Melanie couldn't suppress a giggle. Maybe her mother hadn't forgotten what it was like to be a seventh-grader after all.

In the backseat of the van on the way to the airport, Melanie thought about her mother's comment again. It was true that she had a bigger crush on Shane than she had ever had on Scott, but she had liked Scott a lot. She still did, as a matter of fact. And she knew he still liked her. He had even asked whom she was sitting with at the game last night. So what would he think when he found out that she was going out with Shane now? Or that it had been Shane she was sitting with instead of just some kids from Riverfield, as she had told him?

She slouched down into the corner and looked out the window, but she wasn't seeing the scenery. She was imagining the look on Scott's face when he got the news. He would be hurt. There was no doubt about it. And maybe even mad at her for not being honest with him. The idea made her tingle all over. She really didn't want Scott to be hurt or mad at her. But what could she do?

"Melanie! Melanie! Look at that airplane!" Jeffy shouted, poking her arm with one hand and pointing out the window with the other as a huge jet passed right over their van on its way to land at the airport. "We're almost there!"

Melanie gave her brother a happy grin. She would think about how to handle the problem of Scott later.

"I'll bet that was Grandma's plane," Jeffy chattered excitedly. "I'll bet she was looking out the window and saw our van, too. Hurry, Dad. She'll beat us!"

"It's okay, Jeffy," said Mr. Edwards. "The plane she's on isn't due to land for a few more minutes. We'll get there in plenty of time."

They parked the van and headed into the terminal, arriving at the gate just as the announcement came over the loudspeaker that Flight 306 from Fort Myers, Florida, was on the ground and the passengers were ready to deplane. As the passengers began coming up the jetway, Jeffy turned his head sideways and then upside down as he peered among them, trying to be the first one to spot his grandmother.

"There she is! There she is!" he shouted, bounding toward a slender woman with a deep tan, blondish-white hair cut in a wavy, windblown style, and a pair of sunglasses perched on top of her head. "Grandma Dee!"

"Hi, loves!" Dee Edwards cried, trying to scoop the whole family into her arms at once. "Let me look at you kids. Why, Jeffy, you're getting so tall. You look just the way your father did when he was a little boy. And Melanie! What a beautiful young woman you've turned into. I'll bet you have more boyfriends than you know what to do with."

Melanie's heart swelled at her grandmother's words. Grandma Dee was really cool. She didn't act old like some grandmothers. She knew what was going on in the world. In fact, Melanie thought with a flash, just maybe she would know what to do about Scott. But that wasn't all that Melanie wanted to talk to her grandmother about.

"I'm dying to hear more about parasailing," she said, her eyes wide with excitement. "I'd never have enough nerve to do that."

"Yes," Mr. Edwards said, nodding his head slowly. "I'd like to hear about that, too. Melanie showed us your letter, and quite frankly, I can't believe it. *My mother, parasailing.*"

"What's wrong with that?" Grandma Dee asked indignantly.

"Oh, nothing, I suppose," admitted Mr. Edwards, "except that as I recall, you were never one to go in much for dangerous activities."

Grandma Dee laughed nervously. "Well, let's just say that I'm now in my second childhood. Or," she added, giving Melanie a wink, "my second *teen*-hood."

Grandma Dee sat in the backseat of the van between Melanie and Jeffy and talked to them all the way home about her great life in Florida and all the fun things she did there, including parasailing. "I'm going to miss the Valentine Day tennis tournament," she confided, "but I don't care. I'd much rather be here getting caught up on what my grandchildren are doing." Turning to Melanie, she went on breathlessly, "Now, sweetheart, I want to hear all about junior high. Are you having lots of fun? Do you have a boyfriend? I can't wait to meet all your friends."

Jeffy was sound asleep by the time the van pulled into the Edwardses' driveway, and Melanie had filled her grandmother in on Wakeman Junior High—Grandma Dee thought calling it Wacko was a riot—and cheerleading and, of course, The Fabulous Five. "I'll tell you about my boyfriend later," Melanie whispered, "when we can talk in private."

Grandma Dee gave her a conspiratorial wink and climbed out of the van.

After lunch, Grandma Dee announced that she would like to unpack and get settled into the guest room. "Run along, everyone, and take care of your own business," she said, shooing them away. Melanie was relieved because she needed new sneakers desperately, and it gave her time to go to the mall with her mother.

The sneakers took longer to pick out than she had anticipated. There were just too many styles and colors to choose from. She had liked the gold lamé deck shoes, but her mother had insisted that they weren't very practical. Then she had seen some beaded ones, but the beads were all the wrong colors. She had finally opted for white shoes with "Wakeman Junior High" stenciled across the toes in bright fuchsia.

"Grandma Dee will love them," she said to her mother as Mrs. Edwards paid the cashier.

On the way home she thought again about talking to her grandmother about her love life as soon as they could get some time alone. She wanted to tell Grandma Dee all about Shane, his kooky parents, his pet iguana named Igor, how cool and laid-back he was, and how he looked exactly like River Phoenix at thirteen. Then she would tell her grandmother about Scott and ask her advice about how to break the news to him gently that Shane was her one true love.

When Melanie and her mother got home, they found Grandma Dee sipping a cup of hot tea at the kitchen table. She was wearing jeans and a yellow sweatshirt with a picture of Mickey Mouse on the front, and her sunglasses were still sitting on top of her head. Rainbow, the multicolored dog the Edwardses had rescued from the pound just before Christmas, lay contentedly at her feet.

Melanie shook her head in amazement as she noticed that in addition to a sweatshirt and jeans, her grandmother had on pink-and-white high-top sneakers. Melanie couldn't remember ever seeing Grandma Dee dressed that way before, not when she had come here to see them or any of the times they had visited her in Florida. Maybe her grandmother truly was in her second *teen*hood, as she had called it.

"I'm all moved in," Grandma Dee announced happily. "Jeffy even helped me hang up some of my clothes."

Melanie chuckled. "I'll bet he was a big help."

"Not bad for a six-year-old," said Grandma Dee. "By the way, you had a visitor while you were out, Melanie." Her eyes were twinkling. "Your boyfriend was here, and we had a nice, long chat. I have to say, he's not only handsome, but an extremely nice young man."

Melanie's mouth dropped open. "He was *here*?" she gasped. "Oh, my gosh! Why did I have to go to the mall?"

She sank into the chair beside her grandmother and tried to imagine what it had been like when Shane and Grandma Dee were talking.

"Did you talk about me?" she asked excitedly.

"Of course," her grandmother replied. "He thinks you're awfully special. But then, I think *he's* special, too. You're a lucky young lady to have Scott Daly for a boyfriend."

"Scott?" Melanie asked in astonishment. "*He* was here?"

"Why, yes. That's just what I've been telling you. In fact, I told him you'd be home soon, and he said to say he'd call you."

Melanie sank back in her chair. Oh, no, she thought. What am I going to do now?

CHAPTER

4

Mrs. Edwards poured herself a cup of tea and sat down for a chat with Grandma Dee. Melanie excused herself and started to her room, but just as she passed the telephone on the kitchen wall, it rang.

Scott! she thought, gulping hard. *It's probably him. What if he asks me out? What will I say?*

"Will you get that, honey?" her mother asked.

"Sure," Melanie murmured. Biting her lower lip, she picked up the phone and nervously said hello.

"Hi, Mel. This is Jana."

Melanie's knees buckled in relief. "Hi," she said gratefully. "What's up?"

"Beth just called. She wants all of us to go to Bumpers this afternoon. Christie wants to go, too.

How about you? I know your grandmother just got there today, but can you get away for a little while?"

Melanie's mind was racing. If she went to Bumpers, she wouldn't be home when Scott called. What's more, she hadn't talked to any of The Fabulous Five since her date with Shane last night and their kiss in the backseat of the car.

"Hang on a minute while I ask," she said, cupping her hand over the mouthpiece. "Mom, it's Jana. The Fabulous Five are going to Bumpers for a little while. Is it okay if I go?"

"First Wacko and now Bumpers," said Grandma Dee, shaking her head. "You kids sure have funny names for things. What in the world is Bumpers?"

"It's the fast-food restaurant where all the junior high kids hang out," Melanie quickly explained. "The owner, Mr. Matson, named it Bumpers because he bought a bunch of bumper cars from an old amusement park ride for decoration. You can even sit in some of the cars."

"My goodness, that sounds like a great place," her grandmother exclaimed. "Of course you can go, and I'll go, too." She hesitated, looking sheepish. "I'm sorry, Melanie. I didn't mean to invite myself along. It's just that I'd love to meet your friends, and Bumpers sounds like the perfect place to do it."

"Oh, Grandma Dee. That would be terrific," Melanie cried, genuinely pleased at her suggestion. "I've been telling all my friends how neat you are, they're all dying to meet you. Is it okay, Mom? Can we go to Bumpers?"

Mrs. Edwards chuckled. "It sounds to me as if you *girls* have already decided. It's certainly all right with me. Run along and have a good time."

As soon as Melanie gave the news to Jana and hung up the phone, her grandmother jumped to her feet. "Am I dressed okay for Bumpers?" she asked.

Melanie looked at her pencil-thin grandmother in her jeans and Mickey Mouse sweatshirt. "You look perfect," she said, and then added, "except maybe for the sunglasses stuck in your hair. This isn't Florida, you know. Up here, it's the middle of the winter."

Grandma patted the sunglasses and smiled broadly. "They're just fine right where they are. I always keep them there. That way they're handy in case the sun comes out."

Melanie shook her head in amusement. Grandma Dee was a riot to have around.

A large Saturday afternoon crowd had gathered at Bumpers by the time Melanie's mother dropped them off. Melanie led the way, weaving through the groups of boys and girls, until she reached the corner where The Fabulous Five liked to sit. Jana and Katie were already there.

"Hi, guys. This is my grandmother Dee," she announced proudly. "Grandma, this is Jana Morgan and Katie Shannon."

"Hi, Mrs. Edwards," the girls said in unison.

"Oh, please call me Dee. And I'm very glad to meet you," she said pleasantly as she scooted into the booth beside Katie and took off her down jacket to reveal her Mickey Mouse sweatshirt.

Jana and Katie both rolled their eyes at Melanie, and she wondered if it was because they couldn't imagine calling someone's grandmother by her first name, or if it was because of the way Grandma Dee was dressed. Melanie shrugged back at them. After all, she had warned them that her grandmother was different.

"You've really got a great tan, Mrs. Ed . . . uhm, Dee," offered Katie.

"Why, thank you," Grandma Dee began.

Melanie barely heard her grandmother launch into a story about how she had gotten most of her tan while on a deep-sea fishing trip a couple of weeks ago. Melanie was too busy looking around Bumpers to see who was there. She spotted Laura McCall and her friends in The Fantastic Foursome, Tammy Lucero, Funny Hawthorne, and Melissa McConnell. The sight of Laura made Melanie fume as she remembered how Laura had flirted with Shane at the ball game the night before. Alexis Duvall and Dekeisha Adams were sitting with a big group of girls, and there were tons of boys up at the order counter. She looked quickly for Scott, but to her great relief, he wasn't there. She thought Shane wasn't in Bumpers, either, until she spotted him sitting in an orange bumper car. Igor was in his lap, and Bill Soliday was sitting beside him, feeding the long, green iguana a french fry.

Melanie's heart began pounding at the sight of Shane and the thought of their kiss. If only he would look her way.

"Melanie? Did you hear what I said?" Grandma Dee broke into her thoughts.

"Gosh, no, Grandma. I'm sorry."

"That's all right, dear. I was just saying how I'd like to sit in one of those bumper cars sometime. It would bring back memories. I used to love the bumper car ride at the carnival when I was your age."

Melanie's heart leapt. This could be the answer to her dilemma over Scott. There were no empty bumper cars, so she would have to ask if someone would let her grandmother sit in one for a few minutes. Naturally, the perfect person to ask was Shane, and once Grandma Dee met him and saw how terrific he was, she would be happy to hear that Shane, not Scott, was Melanie's boyfriend.

"Come on, Grandma Dee," said Melanie. She steered her grandmother in the direction of the orange bumper car. Shane had been so busy feeding Igor french fries that she was sure he hadn't seen her yet.

"Hi, Shane," she called out. "There's somebody I'd like for you to meet."

Shane looked up and grinned. "Hey, you must be

Melanie's grandmother from Florida. She's been telling me all about you."

Grandma Dee started to return Shane's smile, but then her face froze as she caught sight of Igor, a french fry dangling from his mouth.

"What is *that*!" she demanded, pointing straight at the iguana.

Shane laughed and stroked Igor's back. "Don't worry," he said. "It's just Igor, my pet iguana. He won't hurt you. In fact, he loves people."

At that, Igor dropped the french fry and flicked his long tongue at Grandma Dee.

"Young man! Get that lizard out of here!" she snapped, and the crowd in Bumpers suddenly got still. "Don't you know that you're breaking the law? There are health regulations against bringing animals into restaurants. I want to talk to the manager!"

Melanie let out a gasp of horror as Grandma Dee whirled around and marched toward the kitchen.

CHAPTER

5

"What happened? Why is everybody so quiet?" demanded Beth. She and Christie had just walked into Bumpers, where everyone was staring silently at the swinging door that led to the kitchen.

At the sound of Beth's voice, soft murmurs of conversation started up around the room again. As Melanie's friends approached the orange bumper car, she blinked and shrugged off the trance that had come over her.

Suddenly emotion shook her. "It's Grandma Dee," she whispered in a choked voice. "She threw a fit when she saw Igor, saying it was against the law to bring animals into restaurants. Then she stormed off to the kitchen to see Mr. Matson."

"Mr. Matson never said anything about Igor's being here before," argued Christie.

A wry smile crossed Shane's face. "That's because he was probably planning to grind him up and serve him as iguana burgers."

"Oh, Shane," protested Melanie. "You know it was because you always took care of him and kept him away from the food."

Bill Soliday picked up Igor's half-chewed french fry and held it between two fingers. "Most of the time," he said and grinned.

Igor's wire cage was sitting on the floor beside the bumper car, and Shane opened it and dropped Igor inside. "Come on, old buddy," he said with a sigh. "We're outta here."

"Don't go," said Melanie. "Grandma Dee can't do anything. Mr. Matson likes Igor."

"Yeah, but your grandmother was probably right about the health law."

"But . . ." Melanie insisted.

"Hey, it's okay," said Shane. "I don't want to cause Mr. Matson any trouble. And can you imagine what this place would be like if everybody brought in a pet? There would be dogs barking and chasing cats, and cats yowling and hanging from the light fixtures."

"Right," said Bill. "Alexis Duvall even has a horse. Can you see that?"

Melanie couldn't help laughing as a picture popped into her mind of the chaos Shane had described plus Alexis's gorgeous Arabian prancing around, knocking over chairs and swishing his long tail into people's food.

"Okay," she conceded. "I guess you're right. You'd better go. I feel awful about this," she said, looking at Shane with pleading eyes.

Shane nodded, and Melanie could see that he didn't want to leave any more than she wanted him to. "I'm sorry I made such a rotten impression on your grandmother," he said softly.

"Me, too," she murmured, thinking that he didn't know the half of it.

Even though Melanie's grandmother hadn't come out of the kitchen yet, by the time Shane was gone, Bumpers was back to normal. Kids were laughing and talking, and music was blaring from the old Wurlitzer jukebox.

Keeping a nervous eye on the kitchen door, Melanie followed Christie and Beth to the booth where Jana and Katie were sitting.

"I just don't understand Grandma Dee anymore. One minute she's totally cool, and the next minute she does something like this! I'm so embarrassed," Melanie confessed to her four best friends.

Jana nodded, then patted Melanie on the arm. "She's still a neat grandma."

"Right," said Katie, winking at the others. "She just has a thing about lizards in restaurants, that's all."

Melanie knew her friends were trying to make her

feel better, and a little smile crept across her face. "I know," she said. "It's just that I wanted her to *like* Shane." She went on to tell them about Scott's coming by her house while she and her mother were at the mall and how Grandma Dee not only thought Scott was her boyfriend but considered him absolutely perfect.

"Ouch," said Christie. "That could get tricky."

"Especially after she got so angry at Shane for having Igor in here," added Jana.

"Exactly," said Melanie. "I just hope I can think of some way to change her impression of Shane."

Just then the kitchen door swung open, and a red-faced Mr. Matson came out, followed by Melanie's grandmother. They both looked around, presumably for Shane and Igor. Then they exchanged words again, and Mr. Matson went back into the kitchen. Grandma Dee smiled triumphantly and headed for The Fabulous Five's booth.

"Well," she said cheerfully, "I guess we got that little matter settled. There'll be no more iguanas in Bumpers. And I see that two more of your friends have joined us, Melanie. Would you care to introduce me?"

Melanie made the introductions and then listened while Grandma Dee told another big story about scuba diving in the Gulf of Mexico and coming nose to nose with a dolphin. Her friends were hanging onto every word, and it was obvious that they were enjoying it. *They* had forgotten all about Shane and Igor. Well, I haven't, she thought angrily.

Loud chatter brought her back to reality.

"It's really nice to meet you, Mrs. Edwards." Dekeisha Adams was extending her hand to shake Grandma Dee's hand. The tall black girl was all smiles, and so was Alexis Duvall, who stood beside her.

"Now, none of this Mrs. Edwards business," Grandma Dee said, shaking her head and laughing. "I want all of you to call me Dee."

Here we go again, Melanie thought. Next she'll be running for homecoming queen. Still, Melanie was glad that the other kids seemed to like her grandmother, because it looked as if Grandma Dee was planning to become a part of the Wacko social scene—whether Melanie liked it or not. And now that Melanie was getting used to the idea, it was neat to have a grandmother who was so with it. If it weren't for her reaction to Shane, having Grandma Dee around would be just about perfect.

"Hey, Mel," shouted Dekeisha. "You guys should have been here after the game last night."

"Right," said Alexis. "Big news! Mr. Matson said he's going to have a Valentine party right here in Bumpers on the night of February fourteenth."

"He said we could even decorate the place if we want to," Dekeisha added breathlessly.

"All right!" cried Melanie. "I hope Shane . . ."

She stopped herself, hoping her grandmother hadn't heard.

She didn't need to worry. Grandma Dee looked enthralled at the idea of the Valentine party. "Goodness, that's only two weeks away," she said. "There's not much time for me to find a date."

That put everyone, including Melanie, into laughing fits.

"Does anyone know if Mr. Matson's married?" asked Christie. "If he were your date, you'd probably get free refreshments."

"Maybe my mom would let you borrow Mr. Dracovitch for the evening, Dee," offered Katie.

"Not Dracula for a Valentine party," Jana said, laughing. "He's strictly for Halloween."

Melanie half-heard Jana explain to her grandmother about the science teacher Katie's mom was dating. The kids called him Dracula behind his back because he wore a shiny black toupee to school and sometimes acted weird to get kids interested in taking his classes. Melanie's own thoughts were on Shane and the Valentine party.

I could hug Mr. Matson right now, she thought happily as she imagined being with Shane on the most romantic night of the year.

Suddenly she sat up straight as if someone had poked her in the ribs. "That's why Scott came by my house today," she murmured to herself. "And why he said he'd call me later. Oh, my gosh. He wants to ask me to the Valentine party!"

CHAPTER

6

For the rest of the day Melanie held her breath every time the phone rang, but Scott didn't call. On Sunday she kept the phone tied up herself, calling each member of The Fabulous Five to talk about her predicament.

"I just don't know what I'm going to do," she wailed, after she had explained to Katie about how she thought Scott was probably going to ask her to the Valentine party. "I really want to go with Shane, but I *can't* hurt Scott's feelings."

Katie had listened patiently, but now she sighed and said, "Honestly, Melanie, you know it isn't fair to string Scott along if you really like Shane."

"I know it isn't," said Melanie, "but Scott's been

my boyfriend for a long time. I can't just tell him to get lost."

Katie snorted. "You don't have to say it that way."

"But how *do* I say it?" Melanie pleaded. "I rehearsed everything before I went to sleep last night, and nothing works. 'Scott, I really like you a lot, but I don't want to go out with you. Can't we just be friends?' YUCK! 'You have a terrific personality, Scott, but I'd rather go out with Shane.' No way! See, Katie? Any way I say it is going to hurt his feelings."

"But you've *got* to say it, even if it does hurt his feelings," Katie insisted. "Otherwise, the mess you're in is just going to get bigger and bigger."

"I know," Melanie mumbled. "But I can't do it yet. I have to think about it a little longer until I come up with the right thing to say."

After they hung up, Melanie called Christie.

"Maybe your grandmother can help," offered Christie. "I mean, she's really cool, and she's bound to have had experience with this kind of stuff."

"*Grandma Dee!*" Melanie exploded, glad in the next instant that her grandmother wasn't nearby to hear her. "She's half the problem. She hates Shane and loves Scott. There's no way she's going to give me advice on breaking up with Scott."

"Have you tried explaining the situation to her?" asked Christie.

"That won't help," said Melanie. "You should have seen her face in Bumpers when she saw Igor sitting on Shane's lap eating a french fry. She'll never like Shane, no matter how much explaining I do. I'm just going to have to think of something else."

"Gosh, Mel. I don't know what to say," Christie replied.

No one answered the phone at Beth's house, which was really unusual, since there were five kids in the Barry family. Someone was almost always at home. Melanie sighed and dialed Jana's number. If Jana didn't have some good ideas, Melanie didn't know what she would do. She was running out of time. Scott could call the instant she put down the phone. Or he might be on his way over to her house at this very minute.

"Come on, Jana. Be at home," she begged as the phone rang for the fourth time.

"Hello."

"Oh, thank goodness you're there, Jana," said Melanie. "I've *got* to talk to you. It's a matter of life and death."

"Wow! What's the matter?"

Melanie went through her story for the third time. "I'll just die if Shane doesn't ask me to the Valentine party, but if he does, what will I tell Scott? And what if Scott asks me first?" Melanie's eyes popped open wide. "Oh, my gosh! I just thought of something!" she burst out before Jana could reply. "*I* didn't know about the Valentine party at Bumpers because Shane and I went straight home after the basketball game Friday night and didn't hear Mr. Matson announce it. I found out yesterday when The Fabulous Five were there together."

"So?" asked Jana, puzzled.

"Don't you see?" Melanie insisted, her voice rising to the panic level. "If *I* didn't know about it, neither did Shane. What if he isn't planning to ask me because he doesn't even know there's going to be a party?"

"Gosh, I see what you mean," said Jana. "And Scott *does* know because he was there Friday night."

"Oh, Jana, what am I going to do?" moaned Melanie.

"Let me think," said Jana. "There has to be some way to work this out."

She paused, and Melanie danced from one foot to the other.

"You could call Shane and ask *him* to the party," suggested Jana. "Girls ask boys out all the time."

"No, no," Melanie insisted. "It's too early. He just kissed me and told me he liked me Friday night. I can't make him think that I'm chasing him. Think of something else," she urged. "Please!"

"I've got it!" shouted Jana. "I'll talk to Randy and have him make sure that Shane knows about the Valentine party."

"Terrific!" Melanie said, almost collapsing with relief at Jana's idea to talk with Randy Kirwan, her boyfriend. "Call him as soon as we hang up. I could be running out of time."

"Right," said Jana. "And I'll also hint around that it's important for Shane to ask you *fast*, before you-know-who does."

"It's not just important," Melanie assured her. "It's *critical*."

CHAPTER

7

When Melanie wasn't worrying about getting a call from Scott, she was worrying that her grandmother would say something about the incident at Bumpers in front of her parents. They liked Shane, but they also knew that his parents were former hippies and that even Shane was a little more laid-back than most of the boys at Wacko. She couldn't be sure how they would feel about his bringing an iguana to Bumpers and feeding him french fries. Fortunately, Grandma Dee hadn't said a word to them about Shane or Igor—as far as she knew.

On the other hand, Melanie thought with a frown, neither Scott nor Shane had called to ask her to the Valentine party. As she hurried to school and the spot by the fence where she always met the rest of The Fabulous Five, she was worrying more than ever about how she would handle her problem.

"I talked to Randy last night, and he said he'd make sure Shane got the word about the party," Jana said.

"Did you tell him it was an emergency?" asked Melanie.

"Well, not exactly," said Jana. "But I think Randy got the message."

"I *hope* so," moaned Melanie. Then she jumped up to attention. "Oh, my gosh! There's Scott, over by the bike rack. Quick, hide me!"

She ducked behind Christie as her friends quickly formed a tight little knot in front of her.

When Scott had turned his back to talk to some other boys, Katie shook her head. "Melanie, you're so paranoid about telling Scott you don't want to date him anymore and hurting his feelings, but how do you think he would feel if he saw what you just did?"

"Well, I couldn't let him see me," Melanie protested. "I haven't figured out what to say to him yet."

The bell rang a few minutes later, and Melanie hurried to her locker and then to homeroom, keeping her eyes down so that she wouldn't see Scott. At the same time, she shot glances around the halls out of the corners of her eyes in case Shane was somewhere near.

After homeroom Melanie dashed to Family Living class.

Scott and Shane were in the class so it would be hard to avoid both of them. She quickly slid into her seat and pretended to be looking for something in her book bag. As badly as she wanted Shane to ask her to the party, she didn't even want to talk to him in front of Scott. Not until she had figured out what to do.

She managed to get out of Family Living class without having to talk to either of them, and for the rest of the morning, she could relax. Shane was in her biology class, but that was after lunch. And Scott was in her last-period English class, but he sat on the other side of the room, by the windows. She could come in at the last minute and leave quickly when the bell rang. That way she wouldn't have to talk to him.

She was feeling a lot more relaxed when the lunch bell rang, and she almost skipped through the hall on her way to the cafeteria. She hardly ever talked to either of the boys during lunch period, because they spent the time with their own friends. But as she hurried past the windows looking into the school office, a blur of blondish-white hair caught her eye, and she stopped short, causing kids behind her to veer around to keep from plowing into her.

"*Grandma Dee!*" she burst out, and then did a double take to make sure her eyes weren't playing tricks on her.

They weren't. It truly was her grandmother, dressed in jeans and a down jacket again, and with her sunglasses stuck in her hair. She was waving her hands and talking in a very animated fashion to Miss Simone, the office secretary, and to the principal, Mr. Bell, both of whom were smiling back at her.

"Oh, no," Melanie groaned. "What's *she* doing here?"

Melanie opened the office door and timidly stepped inside.

As she entered, Mr. Bell looked in her direction and said, "Here's Melanie now. We've just been chatting with your grandmother. She's interested in looking over Wakeman and meeting your teachers."

Melanie tried not to let the panic show in her face. *Grandma Dee had come HERE to look over the school and meet her teachers? In front of her friends? What would the other kids think?*

Grandma Dee looked embarrassed for an instant. "Well, actually, dear, I stopped by to bring this to you." She held out a small notebook, which Melanie recognized at once as her assignment notebook.

"I found it under the kitchen table and thought you might need it," she went on. "And I thought that since I was here anyway, it would be nice to see your school."

"Uhm . . . well . . . thanks for bringing my notebook, Grandma, but it's lunchtime now," Melanie fumbled. "Maybe you'd better come back some other time, when I have a free period and can show you around and stuff. . . ." Her voice trailed off as Mr. Bell began shaking his head.

"Why, Melanie. This is a perfect time for Mrs. Edwards to visit," he said firmly. "Why don't you take her to the cafeteria and let her see how we handle our lunch program. That will be a great chance for her to meet some of your friends, too."

"And have lunch with the kids!" cried Grandma Dee before Melanie could object. "That's a wonderful idea. Besides, I'm starved."

Mr. Bell was nodding now and smiling as if he knew he had just come up with the best idea in the world. "And after lunch you can let her sit in on your classes. It was very nice to meet you, Mrs. Edwards," said Mr. Bell, turning to Melanie's grandmother again. "And welcome to Wakeman Junior High."

Melanie sighed inwardly and opened the door for her grandmother, ushering her into the hall. "Are you sure you want to do this, Grandma Dee? I mean, the food in the cafeteria is really *gross*, and sometimes the kids have food fights. You could end up with spaghetti and meatballs in your hair."

"Come now, Melanie," Mr. Bell called after her. "Aren't you exaggerating a bit?"

Melanie shrugged. "Well, a little bit, maybe."

Grandma Dee stopped once to look at the bulletin board where club announcements and coming events were posted, and a second time at the drinking fountain. She got a drink and grinned impishly at Melanie as she put her thumb over the spray of water and squirted it across the hall.

"*Grandma Dee!*" Melanie cried in astonishment. At the same time, she breathed a sigh of relief that everyone had gone to the cafeteria by now and the hall was empty. Fortunately, no one had seen what her grandmother had just done except her.

"I haven't done that in *years*!" said her grandmother, obviously satisfied with herself. "Come on. What else can we do?"

"I think we'd better just go to the cafeteria," said Melanie.

"I know," said Grandma Dee. Then she cupped her hand over her mouth and pulled Melanie toward her, whispering conspiratorially, "Let's go into the girls' room and write 'Melanie plus Scott' on the walls."

Melanie looked at her grandmother in horror.

"Oh, sweetheart, can't you tell when I'm joking?" Grandma Dee asked with a laugh. She went bouncing on down the hall, and Melanie let out a big sigh and caught up with her, wondering what on earth her grandmother was going to do next.

There were only four people left in the hot-lunch line by the time Melanie and her grandmother reached the cafeteria. Grandma Dee got a tray and slid it along in front of the steam tables.

"Go for the sandwiches if you want to survive," Melanie warned when she saw her grandmother eyeing the meat loaf. "The tuna salad and the hamburgers are the best. And whatever you do, stay away from the mashed potatoes. They taste like library paste."

"Sounds as if things haven't changed much from my day after all," Grandma Dee said with a wink.

As soon as they had gotten their food, Melanie led the way to The Fabulous Five's table. She could hear a ripple of surprised reactions as the kids she passed looked up and saw her grandmother behind her, prancing along as if she were one of them. Melanie thought she would die of embarrassment.

"Hi, Mrs. Ed . . . uhm, I mean Dee," said Beth, and the others joined the greeting.

"Hi, girls. Mind if I join you?" asked Grandma Dee.

"Of course not," said Jana. "We'd love to have you eat with us."

"What are you doing at school?" asked Katie.

Grandma Dee seemed delighted at the question. "Well," she said with a bright smile, "I dropped off something Melanie forgot when she left this morning. And I thought that since I'm going to be staying here for a while, I ought to see Melanie's school and get to know her teachers as long as I'm in the building. I want to be involved and help out in any way I can."

"That's terrific," Christie said. "Not that many grandmothers are so concerned."

"Yeah, Melanie. You're pretty lucky," said Jana.

"Hi, Dee! Hi, Dee!" sang a chorus of voices.

When Melanie glanced around, she saw that

Dekeisha, Alexis, and two or three other girls who had been in Bumpers on Saturday were passing the table on their way to the tray return.

"Hi, girls. How are you doing?" Grandma Dee called in response. "What a nice school," she said to Melanie and her friends when the others had gone on past. "Everyone is so friendly."

Melanie smiled weakly and took a bite of her tuna salad sandwich. So far, so good, she thought, but she couldn't help feeling nervous about what her grandmother might do.

To Melanie's relief, they finished lunch without incident. Grandma Dee entertained The Fabulous Five with stories about her trip to the Daytona 500 automobile race in Florida the year before and some of the handsome race car drivers she had met.

"I'll have to miss the race this year because it's always held in February," she told them. "But that's okay with me. I'd rather be here."

Melanie sighed, wondering if her grandmother ever ran out of stories about her adventures. So far, in addition to parasailing, she had told everyone about scuba diving, deep-sea fishing, and, now, going to the Daytona 500. At least she didn't race one of the cars, Melanie mused.

Suddenly she felt a nudge in the ribs. "Look," her grandmother whispered, pointing across the cafeteria. "There's that nice Scott Daly over there. I'm going to see if I can catch his attention."

To Melanie's horror, Grandma Dee stood up and began waving in Scott's direction.

CHAPTER

8

"Oh, Dee! There's someone I'd like for you to meet," Jana shouted before Melanie's grandmother could call to Scott. Jana quickly turned and flagged down Funny Hawthorne, who was crossing the cafeteria toward the tray return.

Melanie nearly collapsed with relief. "Thank you, Jana," she murmured under her breath.

"Oh, hi, Jana," said Funny. "What's up?" Funny was in her usual sunny mood, and her smile lit up the table.

"This is Melanie's grandmother," said Jana.

"Just call me Dee," Grandma Dee interjected. "I'm glad to meet you. Put your tray down for a minute and tell me how you got the name Funny."

Funny giggled. "Oh, it's just a nickname. My name's really Karen Janelle, but I was a pretty happy baby, so my parents started calling me Funny. I guess it just stuck."

Grandma Dee clasped her hands in delight. "That's wonderful," she said. "Sit down and tell me more about yourself."

"I'd love to," said Funny, "but I have to go. Laura and the others are waiting for me by the door. It was nice meeting you, Dee. Bye."

Melanie glanced toward the swinging doors leading out of the cafeteria. Laura McCall's face was a storm cloud as she and Tammy Lucero and Melissa McConnell watched Funny leave The Fabulous Five's table.

"Uh-oh. Funny's in trouble now," Melanie mumbled.

"Gosh. I hope not," said Jana. "But you're probably right. I didn't mean to get Funny in trouble."

Grandma Dee's ears perked up at the word *trouble*.

"What's going on?" she asked. "I saw that girl with the long braid giving all of us dirty looks. Who is she, anyway?"

"That's Laura McCall," said Melanie. "She's the leader of a clique called The Fantastic Foursome. They hate The Fabulous Five. I think they're probably just jealous," she added with a toss of her reddish-brown hair.

"To make matters worse, Funny is a member of

The Fantastic Foursome, and she and I got to be friends at the beginning of school," Jana explained. "Laura's never gotten over it."

"Poor Funny," added Christie. "The rumor is that Laura makes the girls do what she tells them, or else they can't stay in her club."

"That's right," said Katie. "She can make their lives miserable."

"What!" exclaimed Grandma Dee, raising her eyebrows in alarm. "That's terrible. She'd better not do anything to Funny, or she'll have me to answer to."

"It's okay, Grandma," Melanie insisted. "Funny can handle it. She's been friends with Laura for a long time."

"What in the world for?" Grandma Dee asked indignantly. "I can't see any reason why she would want to stay friends with someone like that when there are nice girls like you five to be friends with. Where did she go? I'm going to have a talk with her."

Grandma Dee rose dramatically from the table, standing up so quickly that the sunglasses on top of her head bounced. She frowned toward the door, but Funny, Laura, and the rest of The Fantastic Foursome were already gone.

"It's okay, Grandma," Melanie said again. "Honest. Funny likes Laura, or she wouldn't stay friends with her. After all, nobody's perfect."

"Humph," said Grandma Dee. She sat back down, but she kept her eye on the door, and Melanie had a feeling that she had better keep her grandmother from bumping into either Funny Hawthorne or Laura McCall in the halls this afternoon, or there really would be trouble.

When the bell rang ending lunch period, Melanie and her grandmother headed for biology class. Usually Melanie couldn't wait to get to biology. Shane not only was in her class, he was her lab partner, and they always had lots of fun.

But today, with Grandma Dee beside her, Melanie felt her palms sweating as she climbed the stairs to the second floor. What if Grandma Dee said something horribly embarrassing to him about his bringing Igor to Bumpers? And what if Shane got really mad about it and never asked Melanie out again?

Shane saw Melanie and her grandmother come into the room, and he gave them a friendly wave and headed in their direction.

"Hi," he said, directing his greeting to Grandma Dee. "Welcome to Dracula's castle."

Grandma Dee's eyebrows shot up in alarm.

"There's Dracula over there," he said, pointing to Mr. Dracovitch. As usual, the tall, pale science teacher was wearing the shiny black toupee that inspired his nickname.

Grandma Dee glanced his way, and her look of concern deepened.

Melanie bit her lower lip. What was Shane up to, anyway? She didn't like the way this was going. Her grandmother obviously wasn't the least bit impressed with his calling Mr. Dracovitch "Dracula." In fact, she was quieter than she had been ever since she arrived for the visit. Melanie was sorry now that she had made such a big deal to Shane about Grandma Dee's being cool.

But Shane was on a roll. He glanced around as if to be sure no one was listening and then went on, "You should have been here when we dissected cows' eyeballs."

Grandma Dee gasped, but Shane didn't give her time to speak.

"That's right. Cows' eyeballs." Shane rubbed his hands together, completely ignoring Melanie, who was making frantic signs behind her grandmother's back for him to stop.

"You see, I think old Dracula sneaked into a farmer's pasture by the full moon. Then he sucked all the blood out of the cows and popped out their eyeballs."

Shane made a popping sound with his mouth, and Grandma Dee jumped three inches off the floor.

"Young man!" she roared. "I don't know what is wrong with you, but I'm certainly not impressed. First you bring that disgusting lizard into Bumpers, and now you try to scare the daylights out of me with some grisly story about a vampire teacher and cows' eyeballs!"

Shane seemed to shrink under Grandma Dee's angry words.

"I'm sorry, ma'am," he said in a soft voice. "I was just making jokes. Melanie said you were really cool, and I thought . . ."

His voice trailed off, and he gave Melanie a helpless shrug. It was the first time in her life that she had seen Shane at a loss for words.

"It's okay, Grandma. Honest," she said hastily. "Everybody calls Mr. Dracovitch 'Dracula,' and we really did dissect cows' eyeballs. Shane thought you'd think it was funny, didn't you, Shane?"

"Yeah," he mumbled, still looking totally embarrassed. "I guess I was wrong, though."

Grandma Dee took a deep breath and looked sternly around the biology lab. Most of the kids were in the room now, and some had even stopped to see what was going on.

"Well, I think I've seen enough of *Wacko* Junior High for one day," she grumped. "I think I'll go on home now, Melanie. Good-bye, dear."

"Bye, Grandma Dee," Melanie whispered.

As her grandmother left the room, Shane touched Melanie on the shoulder. "Gosh, Melanie. I'm really sorry," he said. "I wanted to make a good impression on her, but I guess I got carried away with my jokes. I don't suppose she'll ever like me now."

Melanie smiled sympathetically, but in the back of her mind she was thinking exactly the same thing.

CHAPTER

9

"But everybody likes Shane," argued Beth.

"Not my grandmother," Melanie assured her.

The Fabulous Five were in Bumpers after school, and Melanie had just finished telling her friends about the disaster in the biology classroom when Shane's jokes had backfired.

"But your grandmother seems so with it," said Katie.

Melanie shrugged. "Sometimes she is, and sometimes she *definitely* is not. I mean, you've seen how sometimes she's practically one of us, joking and laughing and talking about her big adventures. Then, all of a sudden, some teensie little thing happens, and she turns completely around and acts like a *normal* grandmother."

Jana nodded. "Yeah. My grandmother wouldn't be impressed with the cows' eyeballs story, either. She hates anything gory or gruesome."

"Right," agreed Christie. "*My* grandmother would probably think Shane was another Freddie Krueger."

"So what am I supposed to do?" wailed Melanie. "I'll just die if Shane's too chicken to ask me to the Valentine party because of my grandmother."

"I still think you ought to have a talk with her," said Christie. "Explain that things look different than they are. I'll bet she'd understand."

"But what if she didn't?" asked Melanie, poking her straw into the ice in her glass. "What if it only made things worse? I can't take that chance."

"Well, you're going to have to do something," said Jana. "It's less than two weeks until the Valentine party."

"Speaking of the party," said Beth. "Has anybody seen Dekeisha? She wants to get together with us and talk about the decorations."

"There she is," said Katie, pointing toward a green bumper car, where Dekeisha sat talking to Sara Sawyer. Katie caught Dekeisha's eye, and the two girls hurried over to join The Fabulous Five.

"Does anyone have any ideas for decorations?" Dekeisha asked as she scooted into the booth beside

Beth. "I hate to do the same old hearts and Cupids routine."

"What's wrong with that?" Melanie asked indignantly. "We want it to be romantic."

Sara made a face at Melanie. "I agree with Dekeisha," she said. "It's okay to be romantic, but let's be original at the same time."

"Maybe we could make it a costume party," offered Melanie. "Couples could come as famous lovers, like Romeo and Juliet or Kermit and Miss Piggy."

"Get real," said Katie. "Do you know how hard it is to get boys to dress up for a costume party? It would end up with nobody here but girls."

Melanie gave Katie a hurt look. "It was just a suggestion."

"And I've got a suggestion for you," whispered Jana. "You'd better become invisible if you don't want to talk to Scott. I think he's headed this way."

Melanie's mind was whirling. What was she going to do? She couldn't talk to Scott. She just *couldn't*. If he asked her to the Valentine party, she would probably end up saying yes just to keep from hurting his feelings. But then what would Shane think? Besides, Shane was the boy she liked. She wanted to go to the party with *him*.

"Hi, Mel. Can I talk to you a minute?"

Melanie looked up into Scott's smiling face. "Oh, hi, Scott," she said weakly. "Gosh, I . . ."

"She can't right now," Jana piped up. "We're having a meeting."

Scott made a face. "A meeting? Here in Bumpers? What kind of meeting?"

"Of course," Jana said, sounding as if it were the most normal thing in the world. "We're the decorations committee for the Valentine party, and we have to have this meeting—*today.*"

"Oh," said Scott, and then he shrugged. "Well, I'll talk to you later, Mel. Okay?"

Melanie could only nod because of the lump in her throat, and as soon as he had gone, she clutched Jana's hand and said, "Wow! You've rescued me again! That's the second time today. You're the best friend in the world."

"Yeah, well, I can't keep doing it forever," Jana chided gently. "You're going to have to tell Scott the truth, you know, and the sooner the better."

"I know. I know," Melanie insisted. "I'll think of something."

Scott had gone by the time The Fabulous Five left Bumpers. So had Dekeisha and Sara, and the girls still hadn't agreed on decorations for the Valentine party.

But that was the last thing on Melanie's mind when she reached home. She tiptoed in through the back door, hoping to sneak up to her room without having to see her grandmother.

"Hi, Melanie! Hey, Grandma! Melanie's home!"

shouted Jeffy at the top of his lungs. Her little brother was lying on his stomach on the floor, propped up on one elbow over a coloring book. Rainbow was stretched out beside him.

"You little fink," Melanie muttered under her breath.

"Melanie? Is that you?" her mother called. "We're in the family room. Come in and join us."

Melanie groaned and scuffed into the room. "Hi, Mom. Hi, Grandma Dee."

"Hello, sweetheart," said her grandmother. "I was just telling your mother about that dreadful boy and his stories about vampires and cows' eyeballs. I can't help wondering what kind of home he comes from."

"Who was that, dear?" her mother asked. "It doesn't sound like any of your friends."

Melanie gritted her teeth. She couldn't lie.

"It was Shane," she said. "He was just trying to be funny. Actually, it was my fault," she added hastily. "I told him how with it Grandma Dee is, and he just thought . . ." Melanie shrugged helplessly as her voice trailed off.

"Oh," said Mrs. Edwards, nodding her head as if she understood. "I should have thought of Shane." Then chuckling, she said to Melanie's grandmother. "Shane Arrington's parents used to be hippies, and they have a little different view of life. I'm sure Shane got his offbeat sense of humor from them."

"Mom, that's not fair," Melanie protested. "Shane's not a hippie, and he isn't offbeat. He's perfectly normal. Grandma Dee just didn't understand that he was joking, that's all."

"Well, I'm sure everything's going to be just fine, dear," Grandma Dee said soothingly.

Melanie excused herself and stormed off to her room. How could everything be just fine as long as her grandmother disliked Shane and her own parents were prejudiced against him because his parents used to be hippies? It was just one big fat lost cause!

A little while later there was a tap at her bedroom door. "It's me, honey," her mother called. "May I come in?"

"I guess so," Melanie grumped. She was still angry about her mother's attitude toward Shane.

"I want to talk to you about your grandmother," Mrs. Edwards said, sitting down on the edge of Melanie's bed. "I know you're angry with her."

"That's the understatement of the *eon*," mumbled Melanie. "She's absolutely ruining my social life." She went on to tell her mother how Grandma Dee had embarrassed her in Mr. Bell's office and then again in the cafeteria at noon, wanting to talk Funny out of being friends with Laura McCall. Next she explained how Shane had been trying so hard to make her grandmother like him that he had tried *too* hard, and Grandma Dee had practically caused a scene in biology class. "I just don't know what she's going to do next," Melanie confessed.

Mrs. Edwards was quiet for a moment. "I think I understand the problem," she said.

"Well, I wish I did," said Melanie.

"It's because she loves you so much," her mother said quietly. "You see, all her children were boys, and you're her first granddaughter. She wants to be with you as much as she can while she's here and be involved in the things you're doing."

When Melanie didn't respond, her mother patted her hand and moved toward the door. "Remember, dear, she doesn't mean any harm. She just wants to be involved."

Watching the door close behind her mother, Melanie thought, Grandma Dee's not just involved. She's interfering!

CHAPTER

10

Grandma Dee didn't say anything about Shane at supper, and Melanie relaxed a little. But upstairs, as she was doing her homework in her room, a new worry began to grow. Scott. How could she have forgotten that he had said he would talk to her later? Later had to mean one thing. He was going to call her tonight.

Melanie drew little doodles on the notebook page and tried to plan what she would do. Maybe she could ask her parents to say she wasn't home.

"Fat chance," she mumbled under her breath. They would never do a thing like that. They would consider it lying, and besides, they had always insisted that the only way to handle a problem was to face it. But how could she face this one?

If only he would start liking someone else, she thought. Then I wouldn't have to hurt him. The idea had possibilities, but she knew it was just a dream. There was no way she could find someone else for him to like.

What then? Tell him I don't like him anymore? she asked herself for the zillionth time.

Suddenly she heard the phone ring, and panic lifted her straight out of her chair. "Oh, my gosh!" she whispered. "It's him!"

Melanie raced to the door and opened it a crack. She could hear her father saying hello. The bathroom was across the hall from her room, and she made a mad dash into it and closed the door behind herself. She stood there in the dark for a moment, listening to her heart pound. Then she switched on the light and pressed her ear against the door.

"Melanie," she heard her father call from the bottom of the stairs.

She bit her lower lip and waited.

Thunk. Thunk. Thunk. Her father's heavy footsteps were coming up the stairs. Then all was quiet for a moment. He was probably looking in her room.

"Melanie?" he called again. "Where are you, honey? You have a phone call."

"In here," she answered. "Who is it?"

"Scott," said her father.

Melanie swallowed hard. This was it.

"Um. I can't come to the phone right now. Okay?" she said, crossing her fingers behind her back.

"I'll tell him you're busy."

"Thank goodness," she whispered to the crack in the door.

Melanie waited until all was quiet downstairs and then opened the bathroom door and tiptoed back across the hall to her room. She sat down at her desk again and stared at her homework, but she was too nervous to concentrate.

All she could think about was Scott. She had had a crush on him in fifth grade, but he hadn't been interested in her then. Or any other girls, for that matter. But finally in sixth grade, things had changed, and he'd started talking to her on the playground at Mark Twain Elementary. Next had come the rumor that he liked her, and finally they had gone to a movie together.

Being Scott's girlfriend had been so much fun, and she had continued to like him even after she and her class entered Wakeman Junior High. But then she had met cool, laid-back Shane Arrington. And eighth-grader Garrett Boldt, the photographer for the yearbook, who sometimes let her be his assistant. She had even been interested in Derek Travelstead for a while. But gradually her crush on Shane had grown until she hardly thought about any boy but him.

Her thoughts were interrupted by the ringing of the phone again. "Oh, no!" she whispered. "He's calling back!"

Melanie zoomed out of her room and into the bathroom, slamming the door and looking around in a panic.

"The shower," she mumbled. "I'm taking a shower."

Turning on the water full blast, she plastered her ear to the door again, but the shower was making so much noise behind her that she couldn't hear a thing outside the bathroom.

She held her breath and waited until steam fogged the room and her face disappeared from the mirror. Surely if it had been Scott calling again, he had hung up by now. She pushed a damp strand of hair out of her eyes and peered into the hall, feeling like a fugitive.

All was quiet, but when she crossed the hall to her room, she found a yellow square of paper stuck to her door with the message "Scott called again" written on it.

Melanie breathed a gigantic sigh of relief. She had escaped—one more time. But how much longer could she keep this up? *Forever*, she assured herself, if that's how long it would take.

She started to sit down at her desk again but stopped to measure the distance from the chair to the door with her eyes. She had been able to make it to the bathroom without any problems both times the phone had rung. But why take chances? she thought. She sat down cross-legged on the floor, her back against the door frame, and listened. There was no use even trying to do her homework now.

Melanie looked at her watch. 8:15. Still plenty of time for Scott to call again. How long had it been since he last called? she wondered. Ten minutes? Fifteen? She had no idea how long it had been between the first and second calls.

"Rats," she mumbled. "If only I'd looked at my watch then, I'd know when to expect him to try again."

Suddenly a sound caught her attention, and it wasn't the ringing of the phone.

"Come on, Jeffy. Quit dawdling around," her mother was saying. "It's time for your bath."

Melanie's eyes bulged in horror. Jeffy couldn't take his bath now! Where would she hide when Scott called?

But two sets of footsteps were coming up the stairs, and Melanie knew she was doomed.

"Wait till I get my toys," Jeffy shouted, and scrambled down the hall to his room.

Melanie listened to her mother hum as she began drawing Jeffy's bathwater. This could take forever, she thought. If Jeffy took his plastic dinosaurs into the tub and played sea monsters, he'd turn into a wrinkly sea creature himself before Mrs. Edwards could drag him out.

Melanie buried her head in her hands. "What am

I going to do?" she wailed. "Scott's going to call, and I'm going to *have* to talk to him."

The minutes ticked by. 8:18. 8:27. 8:32. She could hear Jeffy splashing happily in the tub, but the phone didn't ring. Maybe Scott had given up. Maybe she could put off talking to him until at least tomorrow. At 8:33 she stood up and stretched her arms high over her head.

"*RIINGG!*" The sound of the phone startled her so badly that she almost tripped over her feet. She looked around her room in a panic, but there was no place she could possibly hide.

"Why, yes, Scott. She's here." Her mother's voice floated up the stairs. "Just a moment. I'll get her."

In desperation Melanie took a deep breath and made a mad dash for the bathroom. Ignoring Jeffy, who looked at her wide-eyed from his tubful of bubbles, she knelt down by the toilet and made the worst wretching sound she possibly could. Then she quickly flushed the toilet.

An instant later her mother came bursting into the room. "Melanie, are you okay?"

Melanie shook her head. "My stomach," she said weakly.

"Oh, dear," said Mrs. Edwards.

"But she didn't really throw up," Jeffy said from the tub.

"Hush, dear. Your sister is sick. I'll take care of you in a minute."

"I think I'd better lie down," Melanie said as earnestly as she could.

"But she didn't really throw up," Jeffy said a little louder.

Mrs. Edwards continued to ignore Jeffy and helped Melanie to her room, murmuring consoling words as she tucked her into bed. "You just rest now, dear, and I'll check on you again in a little while. And I'll tell Scott that you can't talk to him tonight."

"Scott?" asked Melanie, faking surprise.

Her mother nodded. "He's on the phone. But don't worry. I'll take care of everything."

"Don't I *wish*," Melanie said half aloud.

"What, dear?"

Melanie smiled weakly at her mother. "I just said thanks."

CHAPTER

11

By morning Melanie had made up her mind about two things. First, she definitely was not going to the Valentine party with Scott when it was Shane she really liked. And second, being able to tell Scott that she already had a date would be the easiest way to turn him down. Of course, that still left one small problem. Shane had to ask her to the party—and do it fast. But she had an idea about that, too.

She dressed quickly, planning to leave for school a few minutes early. There were some little shops near Wakeman that Shane rode past on his bike every morning. She would browse in the windows and watch the reflection in the glass until she caught sight of Shane approaching. Then she would very casually saunter to the corner just as he *happened* to pass by, and their paths would come together. Naturally, he would stop and talk to her. It was a brilliant plan, if she did say so herself.

Grandma Dee was sitting at the table working a crossword puzzle when Melanie got to the kitchen. She was wrapped in a woolly blue bathrobe, and her feet were tucked into matching fuzzy slippers. Melanie smiled in amusement at the pair of sunglasses beside her grandmother's coffee mug. Didn't she ever go anywhere without them? Melanie wondered.

"Good morning, dear," Grandma Dee said cheerfully. Then her expression changed to concern. "How are you feeling this morning? Your mother tells me that you were sick to your stomach last night."

The statement jolted Melanie for an instant. She had completely forgotten her little charade in the bathroom when Scott had called the night before.

"Oh, I'm fine," Melanie assured her. "Guess I just needed a good night's sleep." She grabbed a banana from the fruit basket on the counter and a glass from the cupboard, and headed toward the refrigerator for the milk.

"Well, at least let me fix you a good, solid breakfast," said Grandma Dee. She stood up, plopped her sunglasses on top of her head, and marched toward the stove. "You need to get your strength back after throwing up, and a banana and a glass of milk certainly won't do it. You have plenty of time to eat before you have to leave for school. How do you like your eggs?"

"Grandma Dee," Melanie pleaded. "I feel fine. Honest. Besides, I need to leave a little early today."

"Nonsense. What would you do if you got sick again in school? Or fainted? I remember once when I was in school, Dorothy Throgmorten fainted dead away in the middle of geography class, and it was all because she hadn't eaten breakfast."

Melanie opened her mouth to protest again, but just then her mother came into the kitchen, scurrying around as she had done every morning since she'd begun driving the teen taxi.

"Morning, everyone," called Mrs. Edwards. "How are you feeling this morning, Melanie?"

"Great!" said Melanie, putting as much enthusiasm into her response as possible. "I feel terrific."

"Well, if you ask me, she needs a good breakfast," Grandma Dee said sternly.

Mrs. Edwards took a sip of coffee and nodded. "Mmmm." Then she swallowed and added, "I agree."

"But, Mom. I'm in a hurry," Melanie protested. "And I've never felt better in my life."

Her mother sighed helplessly, looking first to Grandma Dee and then to Melanie. "Your grandmother's right, you know. Let her fix you something to eat, and you can ride to school with me in the teen taxi."

"Nothing's as important as your health," Grandma Dee said triumphantly, taking two eggs and a tub of margarine out of the refrigerator.

"Mo-*om*," Melanie pleaded. "Do I have to?"

Her mother nodded. "You seem well enough to go to school, but I want you to have some breakfast before you go."

Melanie sighed. "I'll eat breakfast. Okay? But can't I walk to school? There's nothing wrong with me. Honest!"

Melanie crossed her fingers behind her back. She knew that her mom's teen taxi was a terrific service, picking up students who lived to close to school to get the bus and too far away to walk. But ever since the episode with Brian Olsen, who rode the teen taxi and had embarrassed her at school with a terrific crush on her, she had avoided riding along whenever possible.

Mrs. Edwards didn't answer, and Melanie knew her mother was weighing the possibilities. She decided to play it smart and keep her mouth shut for the moment. There was no use aggravating the situation.

By this time, Jeffy was coming into the kitchen in pajamas with padded feet and a picture of Michelangelo, one of the Teenage Mutant Ninja Turtles, on the front. He stopped and blinked at Melanie as Grandma Dee set a plate of scrambled eggs and a buttered English muffin in front of her.

"How come she's eating breakfast?" he asked in a sleepy voice. "She never eats *eggs* on a school day."

"Melanie was sick last night, sweetheart," Grandma Dee replied. "We don't want her to go to school with an empty tummy and throw up again, now do we?"

Jeffy thought that over for a moment as he climbed up into his chair. "But she didn't really throw up," he said softly.

Melanie shot him a warning look and muttered between clenched teeth. "Shut up, would you?"

"Well, you didn't," he insisted a little louder.

Fortunately, neither her mother nor Grandma Dee had heard Jeffy, and Melanie gobbled up her breakfast, keeping one eye on the clock over the stove. If she hurried, she still might get to the corner ahead of Shane.

"Thanks, Grandma. That was a super breakfast," Melanie said as she rinsed her dishes and loaded them into the dishwasher. "Now, I've got to run. I really do have to get going a little early this morning."

Her mother had gone back upstairs without further insisting that Melanie ride the teen taxi, so she threw her grandmother a big smile and hurried to the hall closet, grabbing her favorite peach-and-white jacket. The colors looked terrific with her reddish-brown hair, and she wanted to look her best for Shane.

"Are you bundling up?" Grandma Dee called from the kitchen. "It's cold out there this morning."

"Sure, Grandma," Melanie called back. "I'll be warm enough. Don't worry."

The sound of slippers scuffing in the hallway made Melanie cringe. "Let me see," said Grandma Dee as she appeared beside the closet door. "What?" No hat? No gloves? No scarf? And that jacket. It doesn't look very warm to me."

"It's fine," Melanie assured her. "It's warmer than it looks."

Grandma Dee was frowning and staring into the closet. "How about this one?" she asked, holding up Melanie's down ski jacket. It was a bright yellow, and Melanie was sorry she had ever bought it. The color made her face look as pale as Mr. Dracovitch's face under his Dracula wig. She certainly didn't want to wear that jacket this morning.

"It's too fat to go into my locker," she said, knowing that it was basically the truth. With all the other things in her locker, she had to really stuff that jacket in to get the door closed.

"Well, at least wear a hat, gloves, and a scarf," Grandma Dee said resolutely. "I won't let you out of the house without them." Her eyes were twinkling, but Melanie knew that she really meant it.

"Okay," Melanie said. "I'll wear all of that stuff if it will really make you happy."

A smile lit her grandmother's face, and Melanie

was glad she had given in. She knew deep down that Grandma Dee was only trying to help.

A block from her house, Melanie stopped behind a tree. She pulled off her ski hat with the pom-pom on top. It looked great on the slopes, but it was a definite no-no for her mission this morning. Off, too, came the gloves and scarf. They made her look as pudgy as a snowman. She stuffed them into her backpack, gave her hair a quick brush to fluff it up after being mashed under the hat, and took off at a run for the corner where she planned to meet Shane.

She slowed to a jog as she got close. She had to be careful now. If Shane saw her running, he might figure out that their meeting was planned. She wished she had time to look at her watch, but she didn't. Not if she was going to stay alert for Shane.

Half a block from the corner, she slowed again, this time to a walk. Her face was hot from running, even though it was a cold morning, and she was panting, sending little clouds of steam into the air. But if her plan worked, it would definitely be worth it. There wasn't much traffic, and the light facing her was red, which meant Shane would have a green right now.

Maybe I'd better speed up, she thought, but just then a bicycle soared through the intersection. It was going so fast that it was almost a blur, but Melanie was still able to make out the rider. It was Shane.

She stopped in her tracks. "Oh, no!" she moaned out loud. "I missed him! I can't *believe* I missed him!" Putting her hands on her hips, she stamped a foot. "And it's all Grandma Dee's fault!"

CHAPTER

12

Melanie stuffed her hands into her pockets and trudged angrily toward school. The cold wind was biting her nose, but inside she had reached the boiling point. Grandma Dee was spoiling everything. She was interfering, plain and simple.

"She may be cool and with it around the other kids," Melanie muttered under her breath, "but she's old-fashioned and overprotective when it comes to me. So what if I didn't eat breakfast or *bundle up,* as she put it? And so what if I faint in class—which, of course, I won't do. It's not her problem!"

She was so engrossed in her thoughts that she almost didn't notice the boy near the curb. He was bending over, inspecting the back tire of his bicycle.

Melanie did a double take. "Shane!"

Shane looked up and gave her a lopsided grin. Then he straightened up and turned to face her. "It's flat," he said, and shrugged. "I must have ridden over a nail or a piece of glass."

Melanie didn't say anything for a moment. She was doing a frantic mental check of her appearance. Nose—red. Hair—windblown and messy. It wasn't going the way she had planned, but she would have to make the best of it. At least Shane was here—and they were *alone*.

"So, what are you going to do?" she asked.

Shane shrugged and glanced toward the traffic that was whizzing by. "Walk it the rest of the way to school, I guess," he said. "There's nothing much I can do until this afternoon after school."

Shane began pushing the wobbly bike down the street, being careful to stay near the curb, and Melanie fell into step beside him.

"Isn't it awfully cold to be riding a bike in February?" she asked. She had wanted to add, "so near to Valentine Day," but she had decided in the nick of time that it would be too obvious.

"It's not much worse than walking," he said, "only it's faster."

"But isn't the wind colder, too?"

Shane raised an eyebrow and gave her a sideways look. "Not if you bundle up."

It was all that Melanie could do to keep from bursting out laughing. That was her grandmother's phrase—bundle up. And here was Shane, wearing a knit cap pulled over his ears, heavy ski mittens, and his coat collar turned up around his neck.

"Hey, you're the one who ought to be cold," Shane went on. "You aren't even wearing gloves."

"Gosh, I guess I forgot to put them on," she sputtered. In a flash, she whipped her hat and gloves out of her backpack and put them on. In another instant, she wrapped the scarf around her throat. So what if she looked like a snowman? Shane was giving her an approving nod.

"That's more like it," he said. "After all, you wouldn't want to get sick and miss the Valentine party at Bumpers, would you?"

Melanie's eyes got big, and she almost tripped over her own feet. What was happening? Was he actually asking her to the party? Or was he just making conversation? This was the moment she had been praying for. She couldn't blow it. She had to keep him talking about the party.

"So you heard about it, too?" she asked, trying to sound casual. "My friends said that Mr. Matson told everyone after the game Friday night. He even said we kids could decorate Bumpers in a Valentine theme. Isn't that great?"

"Yeah," said Shane. "As long as it isn't too lovey-dovey-looking and stupid, if you know what I mean."

Melanie nodded, but the lump in her throat was

too big to speak around. She wanted to look at him, but she was afraid to, so she stared straight ahead.

Neither of them said anything for almost half a block. Then Shane made a soft sound as if he were clearing his throat. "Did you really mean what you said about you and Scott just being good friends?"

Melanie's heart nearly jumped out of her chest. "Yes," she whispered. "That's all we are now, just good friends."

The pounding in her ears was so loud that she wasn't sure she would be able to hear Shane if he spoke again.

He didn't say anything for a long, agonizing moment. Finally he nudged her softly with an elbow and grinned. "Would you like to go to the Valentine party with me?"

He said the words so quickly that Melanie knew he was trying to get them out before he lost his nerve.

"Sure," she replied, and gave him her biggest smile. "I'd really like that."

"Me, too."

For the rest of the way to school, they talked about classes and tests and the usual school stuff. Melanie tried to carry on the conversation with half of her brain, while the other half imagined being with Shane for the Valentine party. The lights would be low. The dance floor would be crowded with other couples, bumping into them and pushing them closer together. Maybe he would even kiss her right there. . . .

"Well, I'll see you around." Shane's words cut into her daydream and brought her back to reality.

They were inside the school ground gates already, and he was steering his crippled bike toward the bicycle rack and waving to her over his shoulder.

"Right," she called after him. "See you."

As soon as he had gone, Melanie took off running, making a beeline for the spot by the chain-link fence where The Fabulous Five met before school every morning. Her four best friends were already there, and she began jumping up and down and shouting as soon as she reached them.

"He did it! He did it! Shane asked me to the Valentine party!"

"Oh, Mel. That's wonderful!" cried Jana, grabbing Melanie and giving her a big hug. "I told you everything would work out."

The others crowded around excitedly, taking turns hugging her.

"What happened? When did he ask you?" asked Beth.

Melanie told her story, beginning with the three calls from Scott the night before and her ducking into the bathroom to avoid answering them.

"I'd love to have been there when you faked throwing up," said Beth. "I'll bet that was a riot."

Melanie nodded. "The worst part was that Jeffy knew I was faking. He tried to tell Mom, but she was too busy being sympathetic to me to pay any attention to him," she admitted. Then she told them about the disastrous scene with her grandmother at breakfast, ending with missing Shane at the corner, only to happen upon him again when his bike had a flat.

"That was when he asked me to the Valentine party. It couldn't have worked out any better if I had planned it that way," Melanie said in a dreamy voice.

"So, what are you going to do now when Scott asks you to the party?" asked Christie.

"Just tell him that I already have a date, that's all," she said.

"I thought you didn't want to hurt his feelings," said Katie.

"I don't," said Melanie. "This way I won't have to tell him I don't like him anymore. Don't you see? He'll just think I'm popular."

Katie gave her a skeptical look, but the bell rang before Melanie could say more. *You'll see, Katie Shannon,* she thought smugly as she headed for her locker. *Now that Shane has asked me to the party, everything is going to work out just fine.*

CHAPTER

13

To Melanie's horror, Scott Daly was leaning against her locker, waiting for her. By the time she saw him, it was too late to duck away. He had seen her first.

"Hi, Mel. Gosh, I'm glad you're here," he said. "When your mom told me you were sick last night, I was afraid you'd have to miss school today."

Melanie's heart melted at the worried expression on Scott's face. His sad eyes were looking at her as if he thought she might have something terminal. An instant memory popped into her mind. It was the time a few months ago when she'd had mononucleosis—the kissing disease, or so she had thought at the time—and how worried she'd been that she might have given it to him. She remembered also all the terrific times they had had together and how it had been Scott who had given her her very first kiss.

"Thanks, Scott," she said softly. "I just had an upset stomach, that's all. I'm fine this morning."

"Great," he said, and a smile spread over his face like the sun breaking out of the clouds.

Scott stepped aside so that she could open her locker and get out the books for her morning classes. Even though she was looking into her locker, she was seeing pictures in her mind of her and Scott holding hands in the movie, listening to music on her stereo, and doing all the other fun things they had done together. Melanie glanced at him out of the corner of her eye. He was one of the cutest boys in the seventh grade. Not only that, he *liked* her. A rush of guilt filled her heart. How could she possibly hurt someone as special as Scott?

When she closed her locker and looked back at him, he was still smiling.

"Say, Mel. Would you like to go to the Valentine party at Bumpers with me?" he asked.

Like a runaway elevator, Melanie's stomach dropped toward her shoes, and there was a funny crackling sound in her ears. The moment she had been dreading had arrived, and Scott was actually asking her to the party. She was going to have to turn him down. Maybe he wouldn't just think she was popular after all. Maybe he would be hurt. Still, she had to do it. There was no choice. She already had a date with Shane.

She took a deep breath and started to speak, but everything seemed to be happening in slow motion.

"Gosh . . . Scott . . ." she finally managed to get out. "I'd . . . love . . . to . . . but . . ."

The rest of her words were drowned out by the bell.

Scott's eyes lit up. "You'd love to! Great! I've got to go. I'll talk to you later." He whirled around and disappeared in the crowd of kids slamming their lockers and pushing their way to their homeroom classes.

"Wait!" Melanie shouted, but it was too late. He was gone. She looked around helplessly. "But I . . ." she protested, but no one in the noisy mob of kids racing past heard her. "I didn't mean . . . Oh, no! What am I going to do *now*?"

Melanie marched to her homeroom like a zombie. It was too incredible to be true. She had meant to say, *I'd love to, but I already have a date*. But when the bell rang, and the noise in the hall drowned out all but *I'd love to,* Scott had thought she was saying yes.

She sank into her seat, not even hearing the roll being called so that Mrs. Clark, her homeroom teacher, had to say her name twice before she answered, "Here."

She would have to talk to Scott and explain that there had been a terrible mistake, she decided. And she would have to do it immediately, before he told anyone that they had a date for the party. It was too awful to imagine what would happen if *both* Scott and Shane started telling other kids that they were going to the Valentine party with Melanie.

"But how am I going to do it?" she whispered to herself as she hurried through the halls to Family Living, her first-period class. She bit her lower lip and tried to imagine the conversation. *Scott, when I said I'd love to, I didn't really mean I'd love to go to the party with you. What I meant was . . .* No, that was all wrong.

She stopped at the drinking fountain and tried again, but her mind was blank. There's absolutely nothing that will work, she thought.

Scott was already in his seat when she got to Family Living class. She waved at him and took her seat, glad that she didn't have to talk to him now. She needed more time. And she definitely needed to talk to the rest of The Fabulous Five. They always stuck by each other in a crisis, and this certainly was a crisis.

Just then Shane came sauntering in the door. Melanie's heart skipped a beat when she saw him. He always looked so cool and sure of himself. Of course she wanted to go to the party with him instead of Scott. How could she have forgotten, even for a moment, how terrific he was?

"Hey, Melanie," he whispered as he went by her desk. "Are you going to Bumpers after school?"

"Sure," she said, aware as she said it that she hadn't given it a thought until this moment.

"See you there, okay?"

Melanie nodded. She'd be there, all right. Wild horses couldn't keep her away.

Just as Shane moved away, she suddenly felt someone looking at her. Glancing up, she locked eyes with Scott. He wasn't smiling now. But he didn't look angry either. Just puzzled.

Eeeek, thought Melanie. This is getting more complicated by the minute.

"You did *what*!" Katie shrieked.

The Fabulous Five were having lunch in the cafeteria, and Melanie had just explained her latest predicament.

"I didn't mean to," moaned Melanie. "It just happened, that's all."

Katie shook her head. "I can't understand for the life of me how you keep getting into these totally weird situations. You've got to do something. You can't let Scott go on thinking you're going to the party with him."

"I *know* that," insisted Melanie. "That's why I'm telling you all this. I need your help figuring out what to do."

"It seems to me that there's only one thing to do," said Beth. "You've got to level with him."

"Right," said Christie. "Just explain that you'd like to go with him but that you already have a date."

"He'll understand," said Jana when Melanie's expression turned to panic.

Melanie took a deep breath and looked around the table at each of her friends. "Okay," she said. "I know you're right. It's going to be hard, but I'll do it. I'll go to his locker after school and talk to him then. Wish me luck."

The five best friends slapped hands over the center of the table.

"You can do it, Mel," said Katie.

"Right," chorused Beth and Jana.

Christie touched her arm. "You'll feel better as soon as it's over."

Melanie smiled weakly. She'd have to feel better, she thought. Nothing could make her feel worse than she did right now.

CHAPTER

14

The rest of the day, every time Melanie saw Scott in the halls, her knees got wobbly. How could you let yourself get into such a mess in the first place? she asked herself over and over again.

When the dismissal bell rang at the end of the day, she slowly headed for the lockers, feeling like a condemned prisoner going to her execution.

If she had been any slower, she would have missed him. Scott was slamming his locker and twirling the combination lock when she walked up.

Melanie took a deep breath. "Scott, can I talk to you a minute?" she said. Her voice sounded thin and whispery, and she had trouble making the words come out.

"Sure," he said.

He was obviously glad to see her, which made what she was about to do all the more awful. He's going to be so hurt, she thought, cringing inside.

Melanie looked around the hall as if help might be standing nearby. Instead, the crowd was thinning as kids closed their lockers and left Wakeman for the day. By the time she turned to speak to Scott, they were almost alone.

"I really need to talk to you," she began. "Do you remember this morning when you asked me to go to the Valentine party with you, and I said I'd love to?"

"Of course," he said, looking confused. "What about it?"

"Well," she said, and then hesitated, swallowing. "The bell rang before I could finish what I was saying."

Scott narrowed his eyes. "And?"

"And . . . the truth is . . ." she looked at him with pleading eyes, "I'd really love to go to the party with you, like I said, but I have this *problem*. I already have a date with Shane."

Scott didn't say anything for a moment. He stared at the floor as if deep in thought, and then he raked his fingers through his hair. Melanie's heart was pounding. What was he thinking? Was he angry at her?

Finally he looked at her again, fixing her with solemn eyes. "Well, if it's a problem, why don't you just tell Shane that you don't want to go with him?"

His words startled her, and she knew she must have a strange look on her face. "But . . . I . . ." she fumbled.

"I mean, he must know about you and me and how long we've been going out together. Doesn't he?" Scott asked.

Melanie nodded mutely. She was totally flabbergasted. How could he have misunderstood her so badly?

"So it won't come as any big shock to him or anything," Scott went on.

"You mean break my date with Shane?" she whispered.

"Of course," said Scott. "I mean, you were the one who said it was a problem. There's no reason you *have* to go with a guy who's a problem. Not when you want to go with me and I want to go with you."

Melanie stared blankly at Scott. She felt as if she were drowning in quicksand.

Just then there was the clatter of footsteps in the empty hallway, and Bill Soliday popped around the corner. "Hey, Daly. Come on. The guys are waiting," he yelled, jerking his head in a motion for Scott to follow. "Oh, hi, Melanie," he added, and grinned.

"Yeah, I'm coming," called Scott. Then he turned back to Melanie. "Don't forget. Just tell him. And if you lose your nerve, I'll tell him for you."

Scott was gone in a flash, and Melanie stared at the spot where he had been standing.

"Scott Daly, why don't you ever stay in one place long enough to hear the whole story?" she cried angrily, knowing he was too far away to hear. "Why don't you let me explain . . . or something . . ." Her words broke off as tears of frustration filled her throat.

Melanie went to her own locker and got out her peach-and-white jacket. It seemed more like days than hours since she had pulled the jacket out of her closet, hoping to look especially nice when she *accidentally* met Shane at the corner before school. So much had happened since then that the mere thought of all of it made her head spin.

She shivered as she stepped out into the cold, even though she had put on her hat, gloves, and scarf. As she hurried down the sidewalk away from the school building, she thought she heard someone call her name. Turning toward the bike rack, she saw Shane, and he was waving her over.

"Hey, Mel. I'm not going to be able to go to Bumpers after all," he said, motioning toward his crippled bike. "I totally forgot about this flat."

"That's okay," she replied. "I probably should go on home, anyway. Big test in math in a couple of days."

They said good-bye, and she headed for home, feeling terribly depressed. What was she going to say to Scott now? She had put her foot in her mouth twice. If she leveled with him after all that had happened, he not only would never believe another word she said, but would probably hate her, as well. And even if she got everything straightened out, she would have a hard time having fun at the Valentine party after all the trouble she had caused.

Why had Mr. Matson decided to have a Valentine party, anyway? she wondered as she turned for home. If he hadn't, none of this would have happened.

Grandma Dee must have been watching out the window, because as soon as Melanie started up the back steps, her grandmother threw open the door.

"I'm so glad you're home," chirped Grandma Dee. "Wait until you hear what I have planned for all of us after supper."

Melanie's shoulders sagged as she sighed and looked at her grandmother. What now? she thought.

"We're going ice skating in the park!" With that, Grandma Dee began gliding around the kitchen floor as if she were skimming across the ice. "Won't it be fun? I went through the box of old skates in the basement and found a pair that fits me perfectly. Your mother says that the rest of you have good skates, so we're all set."

She looked so proud of herself that for an instant Melanie almost let herself get excited, too. Skating on the pond in the park on a winter night was always fun, and there were usually lots of families there with kids she knew. There would be a warming fire on the bank, and her mother would bring a big thermos of hot chocolate. But still, she thought, and sighed, she needed the time to work on her problem. And she really did have homework.

"Gosh, Grandma Dee, I'd love to go," she said apologetically. "But this is a school night, and I have a big math test in a couple of days."

Her grandmother's face fell. "Can't you get away for a little while?" she asked. "We won't be out late. I want to show you some tricks on the ice."

Melanie shook her head. "Afraid not. I'll go with you some other time. And I'll bet you're a terrific skater."

Grandma Dee's eyes twinkled. "Debbie Thomas and Caterina Witt—*look out*!"

After supper her parents bundled up Jeffy, and then everyone except Melanie piled into the teen taxi and headed for the park. As Melanie watched the van pull out of the driveway, a lump the size of a snowball crowded her throat. She felt so lonely. Perhaps staying home to work out her problem hadn't been such a good idea after all.

Just then she heard a soft whimper, and she looked down to see Rainbow sitting at her feet.

"Oh, Rainbow, you're just the person I need to talk to," she said, kneeling and stroking the dog's soft head. "If only you could really help."

Rainbow looked up at her with sympathetic eyes and then trotted along behind her all the way back to her room. Melanie stretched out on her carpet, and

Rainbow snuggled up beside her. They lay there quietly for a while, and then Melanie said, "I just don't know what I'm going to do, Rainbow. I'm trying so hard not to hurt Scott, but everything I do just makes things worse."

Rainbow rested her chin on Melanie's outstretched arm and blinked her understanding.

"And I *can't* break my date with Shane just to keep from telling Scott that I don't want to go out with him anymore."

A sudden noise caught her attention. It was the garage door opening.

"They're back?" Melanie whispered in amazement. "They just left a little while ago."

Rainbow's ears had perked up, too, and she scrambled to her feet and hurried down the stairs, barking a happy greeting. Melanie followed close behind. She couldn't imagine why her family had come back from skating so soon. They had scarcely had time to put on their skates and go once around the pond.

Jeffy was the first one into the kitchen from the garage. His face was red, and he looked as if he was about to cry.

"Mellie! Mellie!" he cried. "Grandma Dee fell down!"

The next instant Mr. and Mrs. Edwards came sideways through the door, forming a pair of human crutches for Grandma Dee, who was limping along between them. The ski cap with the pom-pom on top that she had borrowed from Melanie was askew, and the twinkle was definitely gone from her eyes.

"What happened?" cried Melanie. "Grandma Dee, are you hurt?"

No one said anything for a moment as Melanie's parents helped Grandma Dee into the family room and lowered her onto the sofa. Then Mrs. Edwards shook her head and said, "She took a hard fall almost as soon as she stood up on her skates."

"I'm okay," said Grandma Dee, waving a hand as if to dismiss it all as a lot of nonsense. "I just twisted my ankle, that's all. Thank goodness I didn't break my sunglasses." She pulled off the ski cap to reveal her sunglasses with the earpieces firmly stuck in her hair. "It's been a while since I've been on ice skates, you know. In Florida we don't do much ice skating."

Mr. Edwards shook his head as he knelt beside his mother and began examining her ankle while Melanie's mother got ice and a towel. After a moment her father pulled a footstool under Grandma Dee's ankle, sighed, and said, "Well, it just seems to be sprained. We can be thankful for that."

"But you'll have to keep ice on it and keep it elevated for a while," warned Mrs. Edwards.

Melanie felt a flood of relief. "Here, Grandma Dee. I'll fix the ice pack for you," she said, rushing to her grandmother's side. "Don't worry. You'll be up and around in no time."

"You bet I will," Grandma Dee said with determination. Giving Melanie a big wink, she added, "You don't think I'm going to let a little thing like a sprained ankle keep me away from the Valentine party, do you?"

CHAPTER

15

Melanie avoided both Scott and Shane at school the next day. It wasn't easy. She got to school just as the first bell was ringing so that she wouldn't have to talk to either of them on the school ground. She turned about-face in the halls three times to avoid bumping into Scott twice and Shane once. She ducked into an eighth-grade social studies classroom between second and third periods when she saw Scott just ahead at the drinking fountain. By lunchtime, when she met her friends in the cafeteria, she was frazzled.

"Melanie, you jerk, you're going to lose both of them if you don't fix things—and fix them fast," chided Katie. She was smiling, but Melanie knew from the look in her eyes that she wasn't joking.

Melanie sighed with exasperation. "Okay," she said, "if you're so smart, tell me what to say to Scott." She dug into her backpack and pulled out a pencil and a scrap of paper and posed as if she were ready to write. "Go ahead," she urged. "I'm ready."

"Get real, Mel. You have to say it in your own words," said Katie.

"She's right, you know," said Christie, and the others nodded.

Melanie knew Katie was right. But couldn't they understand how she felt about hurting Scott? There was no use talking to them about it anymore. She would just have to do it her own way.

When she got home after school, she found Grandma Dee on the family room sofa, with her foot propped up on the footstool again. Crossword puzzles and magazines were scattered around her, and the television was tuned to a game show, but it was obvious to Melanie that her grandmother was bored out of her mind. The least I can do is keep her company for a while, she thought.

"Hi, Grandma Dee," Melanie called out as she dumped her books and hung up her coat. "I'll come in and have my after-school snack with you. Do you want some, too?"

"You bet!" said Grandma Dee, beaming at Melanie. "Doing nothing has given me a terrific appetite."

Melanie giggled. Grandma Dee was really something. She hurried to the kitchen and poured two glasses of milk and dug two chocolate brownies out of the cookie jar. She put each brownie on a paper napkin and carried all of it into the family room.

"Here you are, Grandma. Chow down."

After they finished their snacks, Melanie inquired about her grandmother's day. It had been exactly as Melanie suspected. Bor-RING!

"I've had lots of time to think about things, though," Grandma Dee admitted, "and I started wondering if you have a date for the Valentine party. Have you talked to that nice Scott Daly yet?"

Melanie cringed. That was a question she didn't want to answer. Maybe if she just tried to blow it off, her grandmother would be satisfied and let the subject go.

"Yeah, I've talked to Scott," she admitted, casually picking up brownie crumbs from her lap and dropping them into her napkin. "And to another boy, too. I haven't decided whom I'm going with yet."

"Do you mean that you'd actually consider going with someone other than Scott?" Grandma Dee asked crisply. She leaned forward and looked straight into Melanie's eyes as if the idea were simply too bizarre to comprehend.

"Grandma, there are a lot of nice boys out there," insisted Melanie. "Scott's just the only one you've really met so far."

"Well, I've met the boy with the lizard," grumped Grandma Dee.

Melanie looked up at the ceiling, praying silently for patience. "That's Shane Arrington, Grandma Dee, and he's a very nice boy. In fact, he just might be the nicest boy in Wakeman Junior High."

Grandma Dee didn't reply. She simply folded her arms across her chest and sat back against the sofa.

Melanie saw her opportunity and went on talking about Shane, almost tripping over her words in her hurry to convince her grandmother of Shane's worth.

"I know Mom and Dad told you that his parents used to be hippies, and you probably think he's some kind of weirdo since he has a pet iguana, but he's not. And he's not like his parents, either. Not that there's anything wrong with them. He's just himself, that's all. And he's friendly, and nice, and cute, and . . ."

She could see that she was getting nowhere with her grandmother. Frustration bubbled up inside her. Why did Grandma Dee have to dislike Shane? Why couldn't she mind her own business and stay out of things like a normal grandmother? Her mother's words echoed in her mind. *Remember, dear, she doesn't mean any harm. She just wants to be involved.*

Well, she *is* causing harm, Melanie thought stubbornly, terrible harm to my social life. Why doesn't she get involved with Jeffy? But then she remembered that her mother had also said that Grandma

Dee's children had all been boys and that Melanie was her first granddaughter.

Melanie bit her lower lip and thought that over. Okay, she decided. So she wants to be involved. It's up to me to think of some other part of my life for her to be involved in so that she'll leave my love life alone. She needs something else to think about besides Scott and Shane.

"Grandma Dee," she said slowly as an idea started to form. "You were pretty good in school, weren't you?"

"Oh, my, yes," said her grandmother, brightening up again. "Why, I made all A's."

"Terrific," said Melanie. "Could you do me a favor and help me with some math problems?"

Grandma Dee looked startled. "Well," she began, "I suppose these days they do math a lot differently than we did in my day."

"Oh, it's just simple algebra," Melanie assured her. "The same old stuff. It's just that with all the excitement around here last night, I didn't get much studying done. Now I have homework *and* a test to study for tonight, and I can't do both. It would really help a lot if I could leave my problems down here with you. It wouldn't be cheating, since I know how to do them. I just don't have time."

Grandma Dee shrugged. "I guess I could try. If it would help."

"Oh, it would save my life," said Melanie as dramatically as she could. "You don't know how much it would mean to me."

"It's settled then. I'll do it," said Grandma Dee.

Melanie pulled out an old problem sheet from her notebook and handed it to her grandmother with a couple of pencils, and some paper. She'd done this assignment weeks ago, but Grandma Dee didn't have to know that. It would keep her busy and feeling involved.

"Thanks a million, Grandma Dee," said Melanie. "After supper, I'll study for my test, and you can do homework."

As soon as the supper dishes were cleared, Melanie excused herself to study. She headed upstairs, and Grandma Dee waved the problem sheet at Melanie and then gave her a victory sign.

Melanie was feeling a lot better about Grandma Dee as she closed the door to her room. All it had taken was a little thought. If only my other problem could be handled so easily, she thought.

With a sigh she opened her notebook to the math section and tried to study her notes. She had heard that the math test was going to be a killer, so she had no choice but to study. She shuffled through the pages. Something was missing. The classwork they had done today.

Uh-oh, she thought. It must have been mixed in with the stuff I gave Grandma Dee. At this rate, I'll never get ready for the test, she thought in exasperation as she jumped up from her desk and went racing down the stairs.

Melanie started to enter the family room and then stopped at the door. Blinking, she stared at her grandmother, trying to understand. Grandma Dee was bent over the problem sheet, working the math homework in the light from the table lamp, all right, just as Melanie had expected. But it was her sunglasses that caught Melanie's attention. They weren't stuck on the top of her head anymore. Grandma Dee was using them to read!

CHAPTER

16

"Whoops!" Grandma Dee chirped, whipping off her sunglasses when she looked up and saw Melanie standing in the doorway. Then she sighed, smiling slightly, and put them on again. "Caught me, didn't you?" she asked sheepishly. "Here I was, trying to make you think your grandmother didn't even need glasses, when actually I'm as blind as a bat."

Melanie didn't quite know what to say. Her grandmother had obviously been wearing those sunglasses on top of her head when people were around and then sneaking them on to read when she was alone.

"Gosh, Grandma Dee," she began. "It's okay. I mean . . . You didn't have to worry about a thing like that. You're the only grandmother I know who goes parasailing, and scuba diving, and ice skating."

There was a moment of silence, and Grandma Dee looked down at her hands.

Melanie swallowed hard. "I guess you don't do those things, either, huh?" she asked in a small voice.

Grandma Dee shook her head. "I haven't been ice skating in years. That's why I fell down. Somehow I thought ice skating was like riding a bike: Once you learned how, you never forgot. But I was wrong. Couldn't stand up on the blasted things anymore. And as for those other things . . ." Her voice trailed off, and tears rimmed her eyes.

For the first time, Melanie noticed little wrinkles around her grandmother's eyes, and her heart filled with sympathy as she suddenly understood. It was no wonder she had been confused by the way Grandma Dee acted so with it sometimes and so old-fashioned other times. She had been faking it, pretending to be daring and adventurous all along.

"But why . . . ?" Melanie started to ask.

Grandma Dee cut in. "You'll think I'm just an old fool, but I love you so much, and I wanted you to love me just as much. I've seen so many children act as if visiting with their grandparents were a chore. So it seemed to me that if you thought I was really 'cool and with it,' as you've said, that you'd include me in your life, and we could have special times together. I wanted you to believe that your grandmother could do anything you could do. I guess I acted pretty silly, didn't I?"

Melanie went to her grandmother, dropping to her knees beside the sofa and taking Grandma Dee's hands in her own.

"I want you to know that you're the most wonderful grandmother in the world," she said firmly. "You don't *have* to do all those other things for me to love you or want to be with you. Honest."

Grandma Dee pulled a hand away and stroked Melanie's hair. "But I didn't want you to think of me as just a grumpy old fogey," she said earnestly. "I wanted for us to have fun together and for your friends to like me, too."

"We can have fun together, and my friends do like you," Melanie insisted. Then she added with a laugh, "You don't really have to entertain them with stories about your big adventures. I'll bet you do a lot of things that are interesting."

Grandma Dee was thoughtful for a moment. "I guess I could tell them about the two groups I work with who are trying to help endangered wildlife along the Florida Gulf coast. I man a watchpost on the water, looking for manatees, those big sea cows that look something like walruses. I watch for ones that have been injured by pleasure boats and then alert the proper authorities, who come to the manatees' aid. And I help newly hatched baby sea turtles make it from the beach to the water before the birds can swoop down and eat them. But I was afraid that would sound boring to someone your age. There certainly isn't much action involved."

"Gosh, Grandma Dee," Melanie said with a laugh. "Those *are* big adventures, especially if you're a manatee or a baby turtle. My friends would think so, too."

"Do you really think so?" her grandmother asked.

"I *know* so," Melanie said confidently. "They'll think you're a hero. I love you, Grandma Dee," she said, scrambling up onto the sofa and giving her grandmother a big hug.

"I love you, too, sweetheart," Grandma Dee said.

Melanie and her grandmother talked for a few more minutes about manatees and turtles and Grandma Dee's enormous collection of seashells. Finally Melanie went back to her room. She was glad that tonight had happened. She understood a lot of things about her grandmother that she hadn't known before. So many things that her heart was bursting with love.

A little while later she heard the doorbell. She frowned and glanced at the clock beside her bed. It was a little after eight. Her parents hadn't mentioned expecting any company tonight. But that didn't mean that someone couldn't drop by.

She went back to studying for her test, but her thoughts kept returning to Scott and Shane. She would *have* to talk to Scott tomorrow. There was no way she could put it off any longer. Sometime between now and the morning she would have to figure out what to say.

Melanie was so deep in thought that she was startled when a soft knock sounded at her door a moment later.

"Melanie," her mother called. "Shane's here to see you."

"Shane? Here?" she asked, opening the door for her mother. "I wonder what he wants."

"I don't know, honey. Shall I send him up? Your grandmother is in the family room."

"Sure," said Melanie as her heart began to pound. *Why had Shane come over? Was something wrong?*

A look at his expression when he entered her room was all it took to convince her that something was indeed wrong.

"Hi," he said. "There's something I need to talk to you about."

A chill passed through her. "Sure," she murmured, and motioned for him to sit down on the floor. She perched nervously on the edge of her bed.

He traced a pattern in the carpet with the toe of his sneaker, and Melanie thought she would explode. *What did you come over to talk to me about?* she wanted to shout.

Sighing deeply, Shane looked at her. "I came over to tell you that I'll understand if you want to break our date for the Valentine party."

Melanie's eyes grew large. "What made you think I'd want to do a thing like that?"

"I heard a rumor," he said softly.

"A rumor?" Melanie echoed.

"Right," said Shane. "A rumor that you'd rather go with Scott but you've already said you'd go with me."

Melanie's heart almost stopped. "No!" she whispered in horror. "I don't want to break our date! Who told you a thing like that?" As soon as the question was out, she was sorry she asked. There was only one place a rumor like that could have started.

"Some of the guys were talking after school," replied Shane.

"Scott didn't tell you that, did he?" she asked cautiously.

"No," said Shane. "In fact, I don't think he actually said it. He just sort of hinted around about it to Bill Soliday. But why would he even do that if it isn't true?"

Shane was looking at her, waiting for an answer. Melanie tried to keep her expression from giving away how awful she felt inside, but it seemed as though her face were just a mask that could crumble any second and give her away. There was only one thing to say, only one thing that would make any sense to Shane.

"I'd better start at the beginning," she said. For the next few minutes she told him all the things that had happened and how hard she had tried to keep from hurting Scott.

"So, you see," she finished, "I couldn't just look

him in the eye and say, 'I like Shane now, and I'm going to the party with him.'"

"Why not?" Shane asked matter-of-factly.

Melanie let her breath out in exasperation. "Haven't you heard anything I've said? I just explained all that. It would have hurt him."

"I really do understand," Shane said. "I understand that you're the kind of person who wouldn't hurt a fly. That's part of the reason I like you. But don't you see now how much more trouble you can get into by trying too hard not to hurt somebody?"

Melanie nodded slowly. This week had sure taught her that. Shane had been hurt when he'd heard the rumor, and now she would have to hurt Scott anyway when she told him the truth.

"I think you can be honest and still be nice," said Shane. "You may not believe this, but most guys appreciate knowing where they really stand. Just look at how I felt when I heard you wanted to go to the party with Scott. If I were in Scott's shoes, I'd want you to be honest with me."

"You would?" she said incredulously. "Even if it hurt your feelings?"

"Yup," said Shane, nodding. Then he grinned and added, "I'd want you to tell me anytime you decided you like someone else better than me. Especially if it was Igor who beat me out. I'd pound that little rascal."

They both laughed at that.

"Okay," said Melanie. "I'll talk to Scott in the morning before school."

"Good," said Shane. "You'll feel a lot better. Well, I guess I'd better go."

"Okay. And Shane," Melanie said softly, "you really are the one I want to go to the party with."

He gave her a lopsided grin and then kissed her gently on the cheek.

After he left, she floated around the room on a cloud of daydreams. Shane really was the boy she liked best, she thought, touching the spot on her cheek where he had kissed her. She would follow his suggestion and be honest with Scott. She wouldn't try to plan what she would say. She would just let it come naturally, and she knew deep down that that was the right thing to do.

CHAPTER 17

The next morning she was waiting outside the gate at school when Scott came by.

"Hi, Scott," she called. "Can I see you a minute?"

"Sure," he said, looking pleased as he hurried toward her. "What's up? Did you talk to Shane?"

She took a deep breath. This was it. She couldn't duck it any longer. "Scott, there's been a big misunderstanding," she began, "and it's all my fault. You see, I still like you a lot, but I really do want to go to the Valentine party with Shane."

Scott frowned. "But you said—"

"I know I did," Melanie interjected. "The trouble is, I didn't say it right. I was trying so hard not to hurt you that I never could come out and say what I meant. I'm sorry. Really. I hope you aren't mad."

Scott shrugged and looked away for a minute. "I'm not mad. I was even beginning to wonder if you liked someone else by the way you were acting sometimes, and . . . well . . . it's okay. I understand."

He looked so sad that Melanie wanted to cry, but at the same time, she knew she had finally done the right thing.

"Thanks," she said softly. "And, Scott . . . I know it sounds corny, but I really do hope that we can still be friends. I mean, I really don't want us to be mad or anything."

"Sure," Scott said. Then he grinned. "Like I said, I'm not mad. Honest. And . . . hey! I'll see you around. Okay?"

Melanie smiled to herself as she watched him walk away. She didn't have to worry now about not having fun at the Valentine party. Everything had worked out fine.

When Melanie got home from school that afternoon, she headed straight to the family room. It was time to have an important talk with her grandmother.

"Grandma Dee," she began as soon as they had exchanged greetings, "since you and I are such good friends, let's talk about boys."

Grandma Dee looked up in surprise. "Oh, my. You want to talk to *me* about boys?" Then she added, shaking her head, "It's been a long time since I've had much experience."

"Hey, it's like riding a bicycle," Melanie said, laughing. "You never forget. Besides, you said you wanted to be involved in the things I'm doing. And the Valentine party is coming up, remember?"

"Okay," said Grandma Dee, patting a spot on the sofa beside herself. "Sit down and tell me all about boys. I have the feeling that you've decided not to go to the party with Scott after all."

"Right," said Melanie. "Actually, I'm going with Shane."

"The boy with the iguana?" asked Grandma Dee.

Melanie nodded. "Scott is a super person, and I dated him for a long time. But I know you'd really like Shane if you'd give him a chance," she began. "It's true that his parents used to be hippies, and that his pet is, well . . . a little unusual. But Shane's terrific. He just has a goofy sense of humor sometimes."

"Everyone needs a sense of humor," Grandma Dee said, and smiled warmly. "And I'll admit that I do like Scott, but ever since our little talk last night, I've been thinking about how I reacted to Shane. The truth is, I *over*reacted and behaved like a grumpy old fogey. I acted like the exact sort of person I didn't want to be. I'm sure that if you like

Shane, I will, too. Why don't you invite him over sometime so that we can get acquainted?"

"Oh, I will!" cried Melanie. "I'll call him right now."

"And tell him to bring Igor along," Grandma Dee called after her. "I want to get to know him, too."

By Valentine Day and time for the party, Grandma Dee's ankle was fine.

"I still can't decide what to wear," she said as she and Melanie cleared the supper dishes.

"How about your glasses?" Melanie teased.

Grandma Dee gave her a big grin. "Of course I'm going to wear my glasses," she said. "And probably a sweatshirt, jeans, and my sneakers. Does that sound all right?"

"Perfect," said Melanie, thinking that her grandmother really hadn't changed that much since the truth about her adventures had come out. She was still a pretty cool grandma. "And by the way," Melanie added, "Shane said to tell you he wants you to ride with us to Bumpers."

"In that funny little Volkswagen? Is there room?"

"Sure," said Melanie. "He's leaving Igor at home this time."

When the three of them walked into Bumpers, Melanie caught her breath at the sight of the decorations. She had been too wrapped up in her own problems to help with them, but she loved what the others had done. There were red hearts and crepe paper streamers everywhere, the traditional look of Valentine Day after all. It was beautiful, even if Shane might think it was too lovey-dovey, she thought, and smiled.

Immediately a crowd began to gather around Grandma Dee.

"Is it true that you help endangered animals in Florida?" Dekeisha Adams asked.

"How do you get involved in stuff like that?" asked Bill Soliday. "It sounds like fun."

"I guess we can go ahead and enjoy ourselves," Melanie said to Shane. "Grandma Dee's taking care of herself."

Some of the tables had been pushed back to make a dance floor, and music poured out of the old Wurlitzer jukebox.

"Shane! Melanie! Want to sit with us?"

Randy Kirwan was waving them over to a booth where he and Jana and Keith Masterson and Beth were saving them seats.

"Isn't this a terrific party?" Beth shouted over the noise.

Melanie nodded, noticing that Beth was dressed for the occasion, as usual. She had on a sweatshirt with a hand-painted Cupid on the front, and her earrings were big red hearts that were pierced with tiny arrows. Written on the heart on her right ear was "BETH" and on her left, "KEITH."

Suddenly Keith broke out in a big grin and

pointed to the dance floor. "Hey, Mel. Get a load of that."

Melanie whirled around. The music was blaring a fast song, and right in the middle of the floor was Grandma Dee dancing with Scott Daly. She was bouncing up and down to the music, with her sunglasses bobbing on her nose. She looked as if she was having a terrific time, and the kids around the edge of the dance floor were clapping in time with the music.

"Wow! She's pretty good," said Shane.

Melanie burst out laughing. "I guess there are still a few things she can do like a kid," she said, and she and Shane rushed to join her grandmother and Scott on the floor.

Later Shane took Melanie's hand and led her onto the dance floor for a slow song. She rested her head on his shoulder as they swayed to the music.

"Are you having a good time?" he asked.

"Oh, yes," said Melanie.

"Me, too," he said. Then he lifted her chin and gave her a long, tender kiss. "Happy Valentine Day," he whispered.

Melanie closed her eyes, barely feeling the dance floor under her feet. What a perfect Valentine Day it had turned out to be!

CHAPTER

18

"Hey, you guys, guess what I just heard." Funny Hawthorne pushed her way through the after-school crowd at Bumpers and headed for The Fabulous Five's booth. She was completely out of breath. "It's just a rumor, but if it's true, Beth, you're going to love it."

"Don't keep us in suspense," said Beth. "What is it?"

The Fabulous Five kept their eyes on Funny as she dropped down next to Beth. "It's about the new Media Club. I heard from Dekeisha Adams, who heard from Heather Clark, that Pam Wolthoff overheard Mr. Levine telling Miss Dickinson—"

"Good grief!" Beth burst out in frustration. "Just tell us."

"Yeah," urged Jana. "What did you hear?"

"Sorry," said Funny, giggling in embarrassment. "Well, what I heard is that the Media Club is going to do a show on cable TV."

"Come on." Melanie snickered. "The brand-new Media Club from Wakeman Junior High is going to do a real TV show?"

"That's the rumor," Funny insisted.

"We haven't even had our first meeting yet," said Beth. "None of us knows the first thing about television production."

Funny sighed, and got up to leave. "Okay, you guys. Don't believe me if you don't want to. That's what I heard."

As the rest of The Fabulous Five went back to making plans for the weekend, Beth's thoughts drifted. A tingle of excitement had started up her spine.

What if it were really true? What if she, Beth Barry, actually got to be an actress on TV? That would be show business. *Real* show business. Not just school plays.

"Earth to Beth. Earth to Beth," called Katie, nudging her.

"Yeah, Beth," Jana teased. "Are you still going to talk to your old friends when you become a famous TV star?"

"It would be so exciting if it was true!" Melanie said. "Just think of the other stars you'd meet. And all the great clothes you'd get to wear."

Clothes? Beth thought, looking down at her red stretch pants and the oversized red top with the black and white panda on it. She loved the outfit, but it certainly wasn't something she could wear on television. For that matter, neither were any of the other kooky clothes that she loved to wear.

The rumor probably isn't true, she thought, but if it is, then I'll just have to do a little shopping.

But how much shopping will Beth actually do? Will she be able to stop buying new clothes once she starts? Find out in The Fabulous Five #23: *Mall Mania.*

ABOUT THE AUTHOR

Betsy Haynes, the daughter of a former newswoman, began scribbling poetry and short stories as soon as she learned to write. A serious writing career, however, had to wait until after her marriage and the arrival of her two children. But that early practice must have paid off, for within three months Mrs. Haynes had sold her first story. In addition to a number of magazine short stories and the Taffy Sinclair series, Mrs. Haynes is also the author of *The Great Mom Swap* and its sequel, *The Great Boyfriend Trap.* She lives in Marco Island, Florida, with her husband, who is also an author.